THE BOY IN HIS
WINTER

Also by Norman Lock

Fiction

A History of the Imagination

Joseph Cornell's Operas / Émigrés

Trio

Notes to 'The Book of Supplemental Diagrams' for Marco Knauff's Universe

Land of the Snow Men

The Long Rowing Unto Morning

The King of Sweden

Shadowplay

Grim Tales

Pieces for Small Orchestra & Other Fictions

Escher's Journal

Love Among the Particles
(Bellevue Literary Press)

Stage Plays

Water Music

Favorite Sports of the Martyrs

The House of Correction*
(Broadway Play Publishing Co.)

The Contract

The Sinking Houses*

The Book of Stains*

The Monster in Winter

Radio Plays

Women in Hiding

The Shining Man†

The Primate House

Let's Make Money

Mounting Panic

Poetry

Cirque du Calder

In the Time of Rat

Film

The Body Shop

---

* Published in *Three Plays*
† Published in *Two Plays for Radio*

THE BOY IN HIS
WINTER

an american novel

NORMAN LOCK

Bellevue Literary Press
New York

First Published in the United States in 2014 by
Bellevue Literary Press, New York

FOR INFORMATION, CONTACT:
Bellevue Literary Press
NYU School of Medicine
550 First Avenue
OBV A612
New York, NY 10016

Library of Congress Cataloging-in-Publication Data
Lock, Norman, 1950–
The boy in his winter : an American novel / Norman Lock.
    pages cm
ISBN 978-1-934137-76-5 (pbk.) — ISBN 978-1-934137-77-2 (ebook)
1. Finn, Huckleberry (Fictitious character)—Fiction. 2. Time travel—Fiction.
3. United States—History—Civil War, 1861–1865—Fiction. 4. Reconstruction
(U.S. history, 1865–1877)—Fiction. 5. African Americans—Civil rights—
Southern States—History—20th century—Fiction. I. Twain, Mark, 1835–1910.
Adventures of Huckleberry Finn. II. Title.
PS3562.O218B79 2014
813'.54—dc23   2013049254

Bellevue Literary Press would like to thank all its generous
donors—individuals and foundations—for their support.

 The New York State Council on the Arts
with the support of Governor Andrew
NYSCA Cuomo and the New York State Legislature

Book design and composition by Mulberry Tree Press, Inc.

Manufactured in the United States of America.
FIRST EDITION

1   3   5   7   9   8   6   4   2
ISBN: 978-1-934137-76-5

To my grandsons, Max and Drew,
and for my father, a sailor who has lit out for the Territory

I reckon I got to light out for the Territory . . .

—*The Adventures of Huckleberry Finn*

THE BOY IN HIS
WINTER

PART ONE

July 2, 1835–August 29, 2005

LOOK BACK IN MY OLD AGE on that long-ago day when I came off the river and began my grown-up life—and much earlier still, when, no more than a boy, I set out from Hannibal on the raft with Jim. Of course, I reckon time differently now than we did then, sweeping down the Mississippi toward Mexico as though in a dream. Those days did seem like a dream, though not mine, or Jim's, either, but one belonging to somebody whose hand I almost felt, prodding me onward in spite of my reluctance. Or maybe it was just the river I sensed, shaping a kind of destiny for me and also for Jim, whose end came before mine and was, sadly, neither glorious nor kind. We were, each of us in his own way, looking for something that did not exist.

That other story, Jim's and mine, about a trip downriver, was true enough. But this, the one I am about to tell, is just as true and even more amazing.

You want to know what I mean by "true enough"?

I mean that—regardless of how things might have been exaggerated in the telling, how far the truth got *stretched*—you could always find in the world the same sort of perversity that was set down in his book, only the reality is not so entertaining or picturesque. What I hope to tell if I can find the words and can bear the sometimes bitter recollection is terrible: an abomination dragged up from the mind's reeking bottom like a dead woman asleep inside the closed petals of her sodden skirts. I saw that after the wreck of the *Sultana*, whose charred flotsam glided down the somber river like so many smashed front porches. Mine will not be painted in the garish colors of the book that preceded it by nearly two hundred years.

Whose book?

Mark Twain's, of course. Who else besides him (and now me) has bothered about the fate of two outcasts and runaways: one a thief, the other a slave, both determined to put a thousand miles of river water between themselves and righteousness? We wanted only our freedom. We saw it in different lights, but that's all we wanted. To take the cramp out of existence, to lift our heads above our galled necks and tell all those who said no at every turn to go to hell—or to "blazes," as Tom Sawyer would have said, whose language was more refined than my crude midwestern vernacular, which, in the years since then, I have smoothed out like a wrinkled pair of pants after the hot iron has done its work.

What? You want to know why the story I have to tell is more amazing?

Because it not only happened on the Mississippi River between Hannibal (Twain called it St. Petersburg) and the Gulf of Mexico, along with other of the world's liquid places, but also in time—an unnatural span of it that ordinary mortals cannot hope to cross in a lifetime, or even two.

You'd be wrong to dismiss my book as just another time-travel adventure. While time travel comes into it, the real story, as far as I'm concerned, is what happened to Jim, which wasn't in the least adventurous. No, it was a dirty, stinking horror—a tragedy, if you like the word—that gave me nightmares and disgust for my kind (insofar as I and the rest of what walks on two legs are related by common blood chemistry and a more or less similar shape). I would much prefer having missed it, would rather I had never made the acquaintance of Jim, who was always a friend and who never meant anyone harm. But I'll tell you this: if not Jim, then somebody else. If not a black man, then a person of another color, sex, or affiliation deserving our hatred. Human sacrifice didn't end with the Aztecs, and our civilization has its bloody altar stone buried under a heap of flowers. Enough of that; I don't mean to preach or make my story a moral lesson for Sunday school.

If you were as old as I am and a Christian, as I was, kind of, long ago in Hannibal, you'd likely have sung this: *Be they yellow, black, or white, / All are precious in His sight, / Jesus loves the little children of the world*. It didn't seem right to Tom Sawyer that Injuns, as we called them in our childishness, or Martians, whose complexions we understood also to be red, should have been excluded from the attentions of our Savior. I tended to agree with Tom, though at the time I had no feeling one way or another about Martians. Not long ago, I sat in church in Hannibal and listened while the children lifted their shrill voices in the old hymn and, for the first time, heard it as written: *Red and yellow, black and white, / All are precious in His sight*, et cetera. I suppose in the 1830s, we must have hated Indians even more than blacks, to have left them out of our caterwauling. I wonder if the congregation would have opened its hearts in 2070 to men from Mars, although I'm certain Tom would have, were he still with us. But I swear, there will be no more delving into religion or morality. Not if I can help it—not even if the world should cry out for it and you, reader, grow indignant to hear what certain people consider to be pleasant and amusing pastimes.

Twain hinted at the darkness. I'm just bringing to the surface what was waiting to show itself. Like the woman raised by corruption from the river bottom. Or the light-struck glass plate I saw blooming in the photographer's developer bath at Vicksburg.

You want to know how an unschooled river rat of a boy came to write as if he'd swallowed, whole, Mr. Webster, Mr. Strunk, and Mr. White?

Something of my mythic life must have clung to me after I had left the raft for good. It fitted me, like a keel to a riverboat, for the life I would lead later on as an ordinary man. I'll tell about that in its proper place and time: after I'd concluded my boyish days on the Mississippi, without poor Jim, who was cut down in his prime.

On the river, I'd gotten hold of the truth. At least part of it. So I believed. Maybe I was wrong. Maybe what I took to be the truth—the bitter pill of it—was just something in my mind . . . something I made up. It happened long ago, and I may be only an old man saying whatever comes into his head, as old people will. Maybe it happened the way Twain wrote it, and there was no other journey but his. But then how do you account for what happened to Jim or, much later, my brief and infamous apprenticeship as a dope smuggler and my equally dubious career selling yachts? As I grew older, I found I had a gift for salesman-ship, which is, after all, one of the American arts.

I said that what I had to tell was a horror. But not entirely and not always. Funny things happened to Jim and me, the way they do to all of us. Funny and strange. I'll try to recollect them and try not to let my tune sour. Even small disasters can darken the mind's lucidity, as though the world were seen through a drizzle of dust. It's easy to think of the world as a dirty place unfit for human habitation after you've been in it for as long as I.

ON THE JULY AFTERNOON IN 1835 when Jim and I set out from Hannibal, we had no more idea of heading for Mexico than flying to the moon in a rocket ship like the one I saw shot from a cannon, at a nickelodeon in Baton Rouge, which ended up in the moon's eye. I ought not to have said "set out," for we had no other destination in mind that afternoon than a willow tree drooping over the river as if in sympathy with a universal languor. The heat was fierce. Not the shiftless idlers the good citizens of Hannibal supposed, Jim and I had intended to improve the time by fishing for yellow perch—shy, like us, of the brazen sun. They appeared to be asleep beside a sunken log, pale shadows unmoving on the copper bottom. I know of no more pleasant occupation than to loll peaceably on a raft, one eye drowsing in the latticed shade of a disreputable-looking hat fragrant with straw and sweat, the other watchful for the least submarine disturbance. With blunt fingers, Jim undid a knot of worms from the moist secrecy of a dirt-filled tin can and, separating a fat one from its congregation, set it writhing on a hook. I listened contently as a lead sinker carried the worm down a slant of weakening sunlight toward the perch.

"Care for a cigar?" I asked Jim, producing a panatela from a big satchel where I stashed my movable property. I had none of the other sort, and I always kept the "valuables" with me in case of robbers or Pap, who'd sell them for liquor.

"Delighted," said Jim.

You want to know how Jim came to speak genteelly, as Tom Sawyer would have put it. Wasn't he an unschooled middle-aged slave?

He was. And, in fact, he may not have spoken so

eloquently as he will in this account of our travels together.
Frankly, I can't remember how he spoke in the nineteenth
century—or me, either. I was a boy of thirteen when I left
Hannibal. I'm writing, from a superior vantage point, of
a distant past in which Jim and I lived in a kind of twi-
light country that was neither here nor there, real nor its
opposite. For all I know, we may have talked like lords.
We may have spoken Elizabethan English. But let me say
this—and then to hell with it: Inasmuch as I am the author
of this chronicle, I can, by the prerogatives granted anyone
who hopes to tell even a truthful story, make Jim's native
speech the equivalent of his character, which was sweet
and equable. He was not without his faults; neither of us
was. We were a boy and a man, and neither more nor less
than we should have been.

Having just the one, I cut the cigar in half as justly as
Solomon. The leaf wrapper crackled. I imagined it resented
the knife, which was armored in dried fish scales left from
cleaning a pickerel for Tom's aunt Polly. She liked pickerel,
poached or cornmeal-crusted, but wouldn't allow a catfish
in her house. The Good Book forbade Christian folk to
eat a fish that nature made without scales—a naked and
shameful thing in the sight of God. I licked both halves of
the cigar, which had begun to unravel, then handed Jim his.
He smoked it happily, sitting with his feet in the water, his
broad back toward me. I gazed in fascination at the scars
that spoiled the beauty of skin that looked, in the bright
light and under a fine sheen of sweat, like an eggplant's
in the rain. Too young and ignorant to feel horror or pity,
I saw how a slaver's whip had italicized his strong ebony
back. Jim, naturally, had no idea of the thoughts crossing
my mind. If they were. Maybe my mind was empty while

I sat waiting for a perch to wake and gobble the worm drowning at the end of my hook. It's tempting to imagine thoughts and conversations from those days, which are occurring right now in my head, as if I were a ventriloquist throwing my voice into a dummy.

Like gray worms, the ash at the ends of our cigars grew, unmolested by a feeble breeze that had lain down in the dust, in laziness or exhaustion. The drooping willow branches and the surface of the river displayed unruffled calm. The red bobber marking the end of the human kingdom—although not its ambitions, which recognize few boundaries—would neither bob nor drift; as a consequence, the fishing line (a length of string borrowed from a spool the grocer used to tie up parcels) formed a lazy S on top of the water, while the indifferent fish gave no thought to biting.

I don't know when wind, willow, bobber, string, and fish roused themselves, for it was not long before Jim and I had fallen deeply asleep.

I've been haunted for nearly the whole of my life by the thought that, with a few spectacular exceptions, Jim and I may have slept during the journey. Often, the shore at either side of us looked—well, I don't know how to say how it looked, except like something in a dream. We bore slowly down the middle of the wide river, as if we were driving along a road under a canopy of trees, their fitful leaves shedding a soft glow on the place beneath, a partial light that waved over everything like shadows scattered by the wind. Jim believed that we were under a spell cast by the old woman from Port-au-Prince who practiced voodoo in her shack in the woods beyond Hannibal. I'm certain we were awake during the clash of ironclads at Plum Point and at Vicksburg when the siege was lifted. I have not the slightest doubt we were awake in 1903 when we went ashore at Baton Rouge. The thoughts and sensations I can recall of that night are too strong in me—burned onto my mind's eye—to have been left there by a dream. There is a deep-dyed vividness to my recollection of the nights and days when we broke the river's enchantment and left it, for a while, to walk among men and women whose sorrows were real.

I don't know what it means, if it means anything at all, but at St. Louis—a hundred miles or thereabouts below Hannibal, according to the map of the real world—Jim jolted into alertness and pulled in his line. On the end of it was a yellow perch, eyes fixed on what might have been death, or the glory to come for fish. And consider this: All that remained of our cigars were two delicate gray columns of ash that would not fall from our mouths until we had opened them in astonishment.

"Huck, it was me, Tom Sawyer, who untied the raft!" shouted my friend from another time and place, where I'd been a barefoot, reckless boy and Jim, a barefoot, ignorant, and scorned black man.

Maybe it was only my mind playing tricks or a wayward-ness of sound produced by the unceasing river itself. Maybe I'd gotten myself entangled in Tom's dream. Or in Jim's. How strange and alien must be the dreams of a black man and a slave! How strange my own from those long-ago days! I would not recognize them now.

You want to know if it rained while Jim and I rafted down the Mississippi.

I don't remember, but if it did, then the rain fell as if

its only purpose were to refresh us. It seems to me—while I lie here on the sunporch of what will surely be my last home, save one—that it was always summer then, although I recall snow falling on the river and on the shore, which looked, after snow's patient knitting, like a kind of Russian steppe, but without harshness or cold. But maybe this is true of the weather of childhood, which appears, in recollection, to have known no other season than summer. We must have been sometimes cold and sometimes wet. It could not have been otherwise.

We did not stop our southerly flight (is that what it was?) at St. Louis, because the unholy noise on the broad wharves shamed us. A fat white-coated auctioneer was hammering away the lives of black men, women, and children. I remember his fancy cravat and a dog sprawling in the cool shadow of cotton bales. I remember, also, the alphabet of suffering inscribed on Jim's back when he turned away. I may've mumbled some words of compassion, but more than likely, I kept silent. Of what earthly use would such have been to Jim or to the abject beings standing wordlessly in the insolent sun, waiting to be sold? No, we did not stop in St. Louis in 1835 and would not stop until we got caught by the Little Ice Age, in 1850.

I should tell you about our life on the raft.

WE CAME BY THE RAFT DISHONESTLY, if truth be told, although we did not mean to use it for more than an afternoon. I never could've imagined that, by the time I lost it below New Orleans, the raft's owner, Peter Carlson, would have been dead and buried more than a century and a half earlier.

You're about to object that it did not happen this way. In fact, my story seems more and more inclined to go its own way, with small regard for the truth. Isn't that what you're thinking?

Does anyone really know *how* it happened? Do you? Did Mark Twain? Did it really happen at all? Sometimes I wonder. So when you play the tapes back, make damned sure you type it the way I say it. It's to be my book, after all. Later, you can write your own version. So, where in the hell was I?

Right. We came by the raft dishonestly. We'd only meant to do a little fishing. It was cool and nice under the big willow with its whips trailing over the water. Christ, it was a scorcher of a day! The whole town must have fallen asleep, along with Jim and me. When we finally did wake—if we ever did—the raft was too far along in space and time to return it. We could no more reverse ourselves, our motions in all five dimensions, than fly to the moon. I told you about the moving-picture show I saw in Baton Rouge. It was made by a Frenchman, a magician, whose name I've forgotten—that and a good deal more besides.

Strange, how we can't remember the heat of a day gone by or what a thing felt like—say a girl's silk blouse or the skin of her throat and breast. Oh, a man will say readily enough, "I remember how it felt to touch her breasts. It was a summer night, and she had opened her blouse a little at the neck." Nothing but words. He can't summon the sensation in his fingertips when he touched her or the prickling he felt in his own skin, which may have been the heat of a summer's night but was most likely desire—the yearning of a young man for a girl. Maybe you've noticed it's the same in dreams. You can see, you can hear, but you can't really smell, taste, touch inside them. Some can maybe, not me. Not that it matters for the story I want to tell but can't seem to begin properly. In a story, words are sufficient to bring a thing to life.

The raft. We borrowed it from Mr. Carlson, who had gone to St. Louis to buy a household slave. Looking back, I can't say whether I had an opinion on slavery or not. Household slaves did get to bathe and wear decent clothes, something I never did in those days. Miss Watson and Judge Thatcher kept them, and they were both good Christians, if too full of starch. I wish I could say I *stole* Carlson's raft to spite him for his prejudice. But I already said how Jim and I thought we were taking it for only a couple hours' fishing. Enlightenment in the year 2077 is relatively easy—now that the white race is no longer in the majority. But in 1835, when Jim and I commenced our journey, people were rawer in their sensibilities, more indifferent in their feelings toward others. When my book is published (if it ever is), one hell of a lot of water will have gone under the bridge since I was a roughneck boy.

I wonder if I would've taken to Jim and treated him squarely if my father had been the owner of a cotton gin instead of the town drunk. But I'm digressing—not that I mind. I've always thought you could make a fine book out of nothing but digressions so long as they were scandalous. Have you read *Tristram Shandy*? No? You're missing something. I'm parched—mind getting me a cold lemonade? It's meanness not to allow us liquor, that warm dram of consolation and dreams.

WE ENTERED A CLIMACTIC MOMENT in the Little Ice Age, below St. Louis. The raft was seized, with a noise like needles knitting, and we were hemmed in for winter—river and the old channel's oxbow lake having frozen solid. By now, we guessed that we were not two ordinary river travelers; or if we were merely a boy and a black man, then it must have been the river that was extraordinary: a marvel that protected us by the same mysterious action that had given a common horse wings and changed a woman into a laurel tree.

You want to know if I believe in rapid adaptation—in an accelerated reorganization of atoms in order to rescue what has become suddenly indefensible.

Yes, but not as the ancients did, but as geneticists and machine neuroscientists do now. But in 2077, we have sciences and technologies unknown and undreamt of when, on a stalled raft in 1850, Jim and I shivered with cold and also with a superstitious dread. We worried about our vulnerability, now that the river no longer moved, and with it us. We were like flying insects, in danger when they are still. Could our days on the river have been like a moving picture, creating the illusion of life until a sudden stop destroys it (to use a twentieth-century figure of speech)? Of course, we aired our doubts in terms appropriate to the age. At least Jim did. As I recall, I could find no words for my uneasiness. Always the more articulate, Jim thought the magic that had kept us safe was, by the extremity of winter, overthrown.

Yes, I said *magic*. He believed in it, and so did I. I believe in it yet, skeptic that I am—believe in it at least a little, and a little is enough. We weren't stupid. I may not have gone to school, but I had the native intelligence Thoreau and Emerson admired. So did Jim, who managed, like so many of us, to make room for superstition in an otherwise reasonable mind.

We were scared: Jim, because of the Fugitive Slave Act, and me, because I was in awe of the sanctity of property. Yes, even a hooligan like me. Jim was a runaway, and I was his accomplice. Not that I was above stealing, but my thefts had been of small account. The theft of a man, however, gave me pause and anxiety because of its size. Don't we measure the significance of a thing by the space it occupies? Think of suffering: I believe the pain of a dog to be of a higher order of magnitude than that of a flea. How much greater, then, is the pain of a man? This scale of anguish produced in me a conflict when it came to Jim. On one hand, I sympathized with his misery. He was a man—I could plainly see as much. He'd been bereft of wife and children, who, according to antebellum law, were not his wife and not his children. I understood him well enough to recognize in his silences, his brooding, and in the cries he sometimes uttered in his sleep that he grieved for them. But on the other hand, Jim belonged—by law—to Miss Watson. I hated her, but she had paid good money for him. She had a bill of sale. If he'd been a dog, I'd have gone with Jim "without further ado," as Tom Sawyer used to say. I confess I did not resolve my confusion concerning Jim's status until long after I had left the raft for good and had begun to age as any other human inevitably does.

"I think I ought to go into the woods and hide," said Jim after a lengthy silence in which, doubtless, he had sized up the situation.

He had good reason to vacate the raft, but I hung on to him as you will a rabbit's foot or a cloth doll, for the sake of familiarity and luck. Jim and I'd been inseparable for— how long? From 1835 to 1850: fifteen years. We had covered relatively few river miles together, but time counts for more.

Ours was not the same as now; it was the time of myth—
of childhood, which is not reckoned by any clock, but by
the child, who is a kind of living chronometer. Fifteen child
years is an endlessly long and slow time to share so small
a space with another person, no matter that few could be
found in the states and territories who'd consider Jim one.

"I don't see why you're in such an infernal hurry to get
away!" I complained.

Jim stood next to the ice-locked sweep oar, vacillating. I
admit I enjoyed his distress. I knew he had to go—knew in
the end he would go—but I wasn't about to make it easy for
him. I thought he should squirm some first.

"All right, Huck," he said. "I'll stay."

This was the sort of unselfish gesture Jim was always
making in those days, and I did not care for it. Suddenly,
I saw myself wintering on the raft, a captive to the ice and
to my gratitude. I would be obliged to Jim for having eased
my loneliness at the risk of his own safety. It was too much,
and I turned the tables on him so I might preen in my own
selflessness. What else could a thirteen-year-old boy do?

"No, Jim, I want you to go. I wouldn't want anything to
happen to you."

He smiled and thanked me for my friendship. I shook
his hand and squeezed it to show I did not worry his blackness might rub off. I insisted he take some of the fatback,
biscuits, apples, and rye whiskey with which we'd provi-
sioned ourselves—years before, in Hannibal—for a day of
loafing. We must see to our own needs if we're to be better
off than the sparrow. None of them had lost its goodness,
a miracle of preservation proving we were under a special dispensation. Our supplies never seemed to dwindle.
Whether they were constantly replenished by an invisible

agency or we had no need of them, having no appetite for food, I can't remember. But I was glad Jim took what I offered, else I might have hated him.

"Will you have enough, Huck?" he asked.

"More than enough. And if I get hungry, I'll cut a hole in the ice and fish."

Jim took the food and a demijohn of whiskey and went into the trees. I did not see him again until spring thaw. I returned to the raft and prepared to wait for it beneath a canvas lean-to we'd set up earlier in our journey to keep off the sun.

Was I cold that bitter winter?

I can't remember, though the broad river and the level ground thereabouts brought to mind a snow-covered steppe on which mastodons and Neanderthals harried one another in a remote, equally fantastic past. But surely it was intensely cold, whether Jim and I suffered from it or not. I saw a picture once, painted by Pieter Brueghel, of skaters on a lowlands river turned to ice. This was how it looked on the upper Mississippi in the winter of 1850, when people stepped out onto the frozen river to indulge a childlike wonder at the rarity of it all—their feet shod in iron blades wrought in the St. Genevieve blacksmith's forge.

They paid no attention to me. I thought, at first, I was invisible; but they may have been indifferent in their jubilation and sport to a young ruffian on a raft. In any case, I thought it wise to let Jim be. The sight of a black man in that white emptiness might have diverted them from their pleasure, offering even finer sport than ice-skating. The winter had brought with its chill a kind of carnival abandon. Gray skies were grayer for the bright winter clothes, which were all the brighter for the somber atmosphere. Jim's fresh blood

sprawled on the much-abused ice would have been a color-
ful addition to the scene.

The winter seemed exceptionally long to me, who had
scarcely noticed the passage of time. I thought the blockade
of our raft could account for it. But I did not suffer hard-
ship, except from an impatience to be going on with our
journey, though we still had no idea of its destination. Nor
did I suffer in the least from hunger during my wintering.
I did make a hole in the ice beside the raft and fished for
bullhead and carp, bass and pickerel to moderate my impatience, which may have been only a habitual nervousness.
I was cursed with the jitters, unlike Tom Sawyer, whose
ease and self-possession I'd always envied. I wondered
what had become of him, now that he was getting older,
according to calendars like the one in Aunt Polly's kitchen,
whose pages he'd already have plucked clean—eager, like
any real boy, to escape the serfdom of childhood. The earth
turned relentlessly on its axis for Tom, though not for me.
(I had no inkling of the coming war, in which he'd play his
part with dash, and Jim had not scried it in the bones. But
God surely knew of it and would make certain that the
ground—iron now with cold—would not deny the dead
throngs their lasting rest.)

I must have slept. There was little else to do among the
living while Jim hid. He'd found an abandoned ferryman's
shack and spent his days in speculation, his nights in tormenting himself with the recollection of his family, whose
pain he transmuted into spirituals. They were tinged with
gloom and bitterness, and I did not care for them. I preferred the comic songs of minstrels like the Ethiopian Ser-
enaders I saw with Tom in Hannibal, having crept inside the
tent one summer night. In April, the ice began to thaw, and

Jim came out of the woods. I was happy to see him again, although I pretended unconcern.

"Winter's over," I said as he came aboard the raft, which, like me, was chaffing to resume the southward journey.

"Yes," he said without adornment, the habit of conversation having broken.

A bird settled on the lean-to's ridgepole: a crow, but not even that dire portent had power to move Jim to speech. His jaws were rusted shut by melancholy. I was glad of it, having grown accustomed to silence.

AT CAPE GIRARDEAU, on a bend of the Mississippi between St. Louis and Memphis, the river water, which had fattened with heavy rains in Nebraska and in Iowa, caught up to us. Thick brown ropes of water knotted all around the raft, but we went on, untouched by the upheaval. Around us, the weather was faultless. We lay on the rough deck, sunning ourselves. We might have fished up great whales from the bottom, so magical the day seemed, though the sky above the shore to either side of us was dark and solemn, as if that afternoon were the first Good Friday and we, two careless centurions throwing dice. We would not have known we were in the eye of a storm, surrounded everywhere by rising water, if not for trees, stumps, the walls and roofs of houses, and the bloated cows sweeping past us. That was 1851, the year of the Great Flood. (Another darkness, far ahead and far more terrible, waited downriver for me.)

Yes, I was still thirteen years old. I thought I'd made myself clear. I got on the raft with Jim when I was thirteen and got off for the last time—by myself, for Jim had perished—at the same age. One hundred and seventy years had gone, but I hadn't changed, though my mind must have. All the long while when I was on the river with and then without Jim, I was living (if you can call it that) in mythic time. I know how hard it is to understand; it is nearly impossible for me to explain without resorting to Einstein's general and specific theories of relativity, which I don't understand any more than I understand slow light, time dilation, gravity wells, or black holes. One or another of them may account for the vast span of my existence. (I will not call it my life.) Maybe it has to do with time on a raft, which is slower than that onshore. While Jim and I dawdled our way south, fishing and telling tales, the world on dry land kept another sort of time: that of factories and businesses, of railroads and governments. Jim and I had not so much as a fat gold watch between us. Maybe we were dreaming, after all.

No, we must have been awake—or what am I to make of the chicken coop that, caught in one of the river's ravels, knocked against our raft? A marvel, an improbability maybe, but not a dream. And that was no dream chicken we ate aboard the raft, roasted over the driftwood fire we kept going in a galvanized washtub. Look, I have the wishbone, kept all these years in my tobacco pouch for luck and as proof against the creeping doubt we entertain concerning the truth of recollection. I agree that a wishbone is meager evidence for one who claims to have seen Halley's Comet for the first time in 1835 and three times since!

"What do you believe in, Jim?"

"Luck, mostly."

"Nothing else?"

"Bad luck."

"What about the chicken?" I asked, scraping with my teeth the last morsels of savory flesh from the bone.

Jim shrugged, helplessly, as if the conundrums of the universe were too many and great to be explained by a mere man, free or slave.

"I have a theory," I said.

He said nothing, having become inured to my theories, which were abundant and fanciful. My mind had grown agile in Tom Sawyer's company, though not nearly so creative. Tom was a liar, mostly, while I hope to be truthful.

"I don't think we are any longer in life," I said.

"You mean we're dead?"

I could see that the idea didn't appeal to Jim, who looked around wildly, as if expecting to see a fraternity of ghosts or, at the very least, the yellow dog that had died in the schoolyard, chasing its tail and foaming at the mouth. Had Jim worried about the persistence of rabies in the afterlife of a dog, I'd have assured him that glory, however brief, would have purged it of distemper. But Jim said nothing on the subject.

"No, we ain't dead." (If we'd had this conversation, I was sure to have said *ain't*. Even so illustrious a citizen as Judge Thatcher employed the vernacular on occasion.) "We're cut off, like two flies trapped in amber." (I might have said *marmalade,* but the meaning is the same.)

Jim didn't care for this trope, either. He preferred to avoid the quicksand of metaphysics, which I considered great sport. His mind was more straightforward, if kinked by superstitions.

"I want to try an experiment, Jim."

He looked at me, his sad eyes full of suspicion and hurt. I knew he was thinking of the last experiment, when I'd tried to teach him to swim by shoving him off the raft. Contrary to my earnest expectations, he did not suddenly acquire the gift of flotation and, if not for a passing log fallen off a lumber raft, Jim would have gone straight to the bottom. He clutched, and I pulled him safely up.

"I want to see whether we might not have the power of resurrection," I said.

"I saw Marie Laveau bring a frog back to life once," he said.

I dismissed a frog as too low a creature to prove anything. I pointed, instead, to a dead cow, sailing belly-up on our starboard side, within reach of the boat hook, which I handed to Jim, his arms being longer and considerably stronger than mine.

"Just touch this to the belly of that poor beast. If my theory is correct, it'll come straightaway to life."

Jim did as I asked, even if he muttered some, while I held on to his pants with one hand and the lean-to with the other to ground the corpse in our miraculous energy. (A boy of the twenty-first century would have said *force field*.) If I was right, we'd have plenty of fresh milk for our voyage. The cow, however, continued in the intractability of death. Jim looked relieved. Plainly disgusted, he swished the end of the boat hook in the water to rid it of corruption and evil spirits. The cow did stink.

Did I believe in evil spirits? Hard to say now. But I did believe in evil men, and women. I was impartial, generally speaking, in my low opinion of both sexes. I had only to think of Delilah and Potiphar's wife. And in my experience, there was no more mean-spirited, foul-tempered, sharp-tongued harridan than pious old Miss Watson, who was a woman, of sorts.

I had no adequate theory to explain why the raft was able to travel through time. The water at the river's source,

Minnesota's Lake Itasca, was also traveling into the future. For all I know, it may go on forever and, with it, the piece of river that had seized our raft and held us fast in timelessness. Do you think that's a plausible explanation?

I know the river flows into the Gulf of Mexico! I don't need you to give me a lesson in the geography of the Mississippi Delta. I got soaked to the skin with it. But the water—braiding and unbraiding for more than two thousand miles before finally entering the Gulf—doesn't just stop. It goes on and on. Our raft, in that water, may have been a kind of time machine carried by a freak of nature (*singularity,* to use a modern term)—an unrepeatable combination of circumstances—toward time's distant unfolding, which it never reached because of the damned hurricane.

What is it now? You want to know if we slept.

Naturally, I've said as much. We slept in the ordinary way of men, or a man and a boy. Days alternated with nights, good weather with bad. Only in memory do the conditions of our life on the Mississippi appear uncommon. We may have been surprised, but in those days we accepted magic; we took miracles in stride. When we ventured onto land is another story, which sometimes appalled us. If all seems now to have been a dream, it is only recollection that makes it so. Would it have been a waste and a pity if it had been a dream? I, for one, have spent the best part of my life in dreaming and have profited by it. I've been cheered and uplifted—especially now, in the winter of my life. Even nightmares have something to tell us about ourselves. And inasmuch as dreaming is an aspect of human life, we ought not to reject it.

And if it had been no more than a virtual journey, well—what do *you* say? You're a young man and have more experience with this sort of thing, although I'm deft at raising online maps from the swamp of data. You were born into the Digital Age, while I spent my formative years in the Age of Steam, which I miss. It had its familiars, gods, and avatars, such as the locomotive, the steamboat, the primitive automobile, as well as that most genial altar of the age: the old-fashioned cast-iron radiator, to replace the ancient hearth. For all its speed and efficiency, feats of memory and logic, the computer cannot warm you on a winter's night and—its processes being invisible and all but silent—there's nothing to see and very little to adore.

WE LEFT CAPE GIRARDEAU and the year 1851 behind, and next morning, not long after first light, we made New Madrid, at Missouri's southeastern heel. I watched in fascination as Jim, leaning into the brightness of the newly risen sun, seemed to be eaten by it—first his head and then the balance of him, until he was nothing but an engulfing light—or so it seemed to eyes widened by the recent night.

"You look like a ghost," I said, shifting my gaze because my eyes were stinging the way they will when you step out of darkness into daylight.

Jim was afraid of ghosts and all other tokens of the unseen, which to him was a teeming place fraught with menace. (It must be the same for a virologist.) He was a Christian, but his Baptist faith had become confused with voodoo, as practiced by old Mambo Laveau, who could animate the dead.

"Do you believe in ghosts, Jim?" I asked, to needle him.

"I do."

I shivered to hear his voice, tremulous and thrilling, issue from the temporary dark. I recalled how Tom had scared poor Jim out of his wits by removing the mirror from Miss Watson's chifforobe. When Jim came to make up the fire (his eyes, like mine now, nearly useless after chopping wood in the glaring sun), Tom began to moan hideously. He'd draped himself in a sheet and floured his face, and when he climbed through the mirror's empty frame into Miss Watson's bedroom, Jim fainted dead away. According to voodoo, mirrors are passageways between the living world and the next. At the time, I didn't feel the least sorry for Jim, thinking it only right that someone ignorant enough to believe in the resurrection of frogs, in zombies, and in other perversions of sense should suffer the consequences.

New Madrid floated past us—that is to say, we floated past New Madrid, which the town's boosters claim is the oldest American city west of the Mississippi. Maybe it is; I never bothered to check. A lifetime isn't long enough to verify the countless truths of this world—not even a lifetime as long as mine. My eyes grown accustomed to the new light, I turned once more and looked at Jim, who had reassembled himself in the stern of the raft.

"Ever hear of the 1811 New Madrid earthquake?"

I took every opportunity to sound the depth of Jim's ignorance; such is the cruelty of boys.

"No," he said. Jim was smart, but he had no learning to speak of.

The water that rose in 1811 after the earthquake, flooding fields and streets all the way to the Gulf of Mexico—where is it now? Time, imprinted on its atoms, must have commingled with the Gulf, flavoring it with the past, before seeping to earth's far corners. Much later, did a Fiji islander wash her clothes in antebellum Mississippi River water? Did a woman from Ceylon or Sicily? Did a kayak on Baffin

Bay slip through water that had been stirred, centuries earlier, by the paddle wheel of a Mississippi steamboat? I seem helpless not to think about time, and what I had intended to be a simple story of Jim's and my life on the river becomes more and more snarled in complexity.

Seeing a gaudy paddle wheeler near the opposite shore, I found my thoughts wandering to the pleasures of a journey by boat, instead of toiling aboard a raft. We did often struggle, Jim and I, no matter that we traveled in mythic time toward the future.

ON MAY 10, 1862, WE ARRIVED at Plum Point Bend, where a naval engagement between the Confederate River Defense Fleet and a squadron of Union ironclads was in noisy progress. I should describe the ships' maneuvering, the skirmishing of men on either side, the confusion and alarms. I ought to give an account of the battle's importance, and because the American Civil War is relatively ancient history, I should summarize its causes (having more to do with Jim and his family than with me and mine). But at this moment, I prefer to note the color of the water, the behavior of clouds and cannon smoke in the changeable wind, the elegant figures traced by birds against the reeling sky.

You say I have a duty to history.

Having been in history as long as I have relieves me of any further obligation to it.

You say I have a duty to readers to flesh out my story.

Sorry, but I find such fleshing-out to be tedious and beside the point.

You want to know what my point is in all this?

I'm not sure. You see I am, at least, honest. But I think

"all this" has to do with ideas of time and the secret conflu-
ences by which we arrive at points in our own histories.
But because I do not wish to be remembered (if I will be
remembered) as a self-indulgent fantasist, I'll skip the purple patch for now, however much I wish to write it. I need
to make amends for my indifference, for having turned my
back on the world in favor of the beauties of the way. I'll
try to study cruelty (I regret my own) and render it in more
familiar terms. But something of Mark Twain's playfulness,
his habit of fantasizing and exaggerating must have rubbed
off on me. How could it be otherwise? So this account of
my life must be impure: a mixture of high-minded tragedy
and lowborn comedy. At Plum Point, at this moment in
time, I was more interested in the rude clash of ships and
ironclads than in grand ideas or my moral misdeeds and
childish stupidity. (How could I have imagined that—215
years in the future—I'd be preparing to leave time once
more and, in all probability, never come back to it?) I had
the smell of gunpowder up my nose, and no other smell is
so exciting to the boyish imagination.

Yes, yes! I am an old man and may have forgotten how
the scent of a woman has power to inflame! But if you're
to be the secretary of my memories, you had better learn
to flatter me. I'd have used a Dictaphone, but I dislike
machinery that does not hum or clank—crude sounds that
give it humanity.

Plum Point.

The *General Sumter* had rammed and driven off the
Union ironclad *Cincinnati*. I'd seen the *General Sumter*
many times before, on the river near Hannibal, when she
was the *Junius Beebe,* a side-wheeled steamer working as a
tow. She'd been outfitted in Algiers, Louisiana, with iron

plates covering her bow and commissioned as a ram for the Confederacy. She was giving the Union boats hell, and I had my hat off to her when the *Cincinnati* ran aground. I could see Jim didn't approve of my enthusiasm, but at the time I thought no more of the skirmish than if I'd witnessed a contest of battling eggs or a ruckus in the schoolyard. My conscience was raw and unformed.

On the *General Sumter*, three Confederate officers were leaning on the upper-deck railing, when one of them straightened up and began to shout toward us, "Ahoy! Huckleberry Finn!"

He and I might have been parted by fifty yards of water and twenty-seven years when we'd gone our separate ways, but I knew at once and without doubt that the officer waving to me was Tom Sawyer! He climbed down the ladder onto the lower deck and, shortly, was making toward us in a skiff rowed by two rebel sailors. Jim was in a panic, for he could expect nothing but the whip and the shackle from representatives of Jeff Davis's government. And I couldn't be sure that Tom hadn't become a dyed-in-the-wool Confederate since I had seen him last; he came from Missouri and had grown up surrounded by slaves who called him "young master."

"Play dead, Jim," I said.

Jim fell facedown onto the raft, where he gave a convincing portrayal of a man departed from this earth. I never did fathom how, in that desperate moment, he had managed to suppress the natural shiver that comes to a human being in fear for his life. I threw a blanket over his head and laid a piece of fatback on his naked back. It looked just like mutilated flesh, and to complete the illusion, I pried open the tin can where we kept putrefied chicken gizzards, a sovereign bait for catching catfish. As the skiff pulled alongside, Tom and his crew hesitated in the presence of so formidable a stink. I had my knife and appeared to be cutting a strip of meat from Jim, as though hunger had driven me to the extremity of cannibalism.

"Hello, Huck," said Tom, eyeing me with a look of profound disappointment at how low I had fallen. "Are you eating that n———?"

"I am, Tom," I said. "Hunger's made me do it." I cut off another strip of pinkish meat, put it in my mouth, and chewed noisily. Jim never moved a muscle.

One of the sailors vomited over the side of the skiff. I was pleased to see that my theatrics were appreciated. (Wasn't the raft a kind of stage on which we played parts assigned to us by someone else?)

"Might that be Jim you're dining on?" Tom asked.

"It is," I said. "He keeled over day before yesterday of starvation. His last words to me were to eat him before he spoiled."

"Smells like he's gone off some," said Tom, his finely shaped nose hunting the air as if for the departing atoms of his childhood, instead of the deceased slave he'd frequently bedeviled.

"Hotter than usual for the time of year—don't you think so, Tom?"

He nodded in agreement, and I admired how well he had grown into a man. He had dash, and his looks had ripened into a dark handsomeness. At thirty-eight, he looked about as striking as a man can in a Confederate uniform.

"Jim was a good n———," he said. "Makes me glad to see him dead, else I'd have had to hang him for a runaway."

I thought for sure Jim would scream or make a

commotion, but he didn't—aware, doubtless, of the gravity of his situation.

"Care for some?" I asked, indicating the place on Jim's back I'd been carving.

"No, thank you, Huck," said Tom, with the nice manners of an officer and a gentleman.

"How 'bout you boys? Care for some dead n———?" I was sure Jim would forgive me for using that hateful word in the name of verisimilitude.

I am not one to curry favor, but for Jim's sake, I smiled at the pair of Mississippians; for so I knew them to be from the timbre of their voices. They refused me. Fortunately, not one of the three men in gray showed any desire to take a look at Jim's face hidden under the blanket.

"You don't look a day older, Huck," said Tom, who bore his early middle age splendidly.

"I'm still only thirteen," I said.

"How's that?"

"Don't know," I said.

Our conversation was suddenly becalmed, but Tom seemed reluctant to go. He and I had been the best of friends, and maybe he thought we should speak fondly of the days of our common boyhood on the wharves and mudflats of Hannibal. But apparently he could find nothing more to say. As for me, I was nervously waiting for him and his oarsmen to be gone. Just then, a bell rang out merrily on the *General Sumter*.

"Lunch is ready!" said Tom, suddenly discovering his appetite. "Row us back to the boat, boys," he said, taking his seat in the stern. "It was swell to see you again, Huck."

"Same here, Tom."

"You take good care, now."

"I'll try," I said.

And then Tom was gone from our lives, and Jim could breathe once again like a living man.

I said earlier that I would avoid the vernacular in favor of a more dignified way of speaking. But I couldn't resist it and may fall, again, into a common usage for the fun of it. The only person who might object to my attempts at dialect is Jim, and he's long dead.

"I HATE WHEN YOU SIT and brood, Jim."

"I don't brood; I think."

"What do you think about?"

"At night, I think about the origin of stars: how they hurl themselves against the outposts of nothingness. During the day, of the effects of sunlight on fog and water, the secret language of birds and how they turn as one in flight, and how a cloud of gnats reproduces certain nebula in miniature."

I feel obliged to rehabilitate Jim after having shown him in less than a heroic light during the performance of our theater of cannibalism. He was not the simpleton Mark Twain made him out to be, nor was he the blank, the zero, the empty slate I sometimes took him for. It isn't easy to describe well and truly the persons and events that figured in my story. I've scribbled some before, but not at length or with a responsibility to my characters—which, in this instance, are Jim and I.

To continue our palaver, without the artifice of dialect to make it plausible:

"What do you dream, Jim?"

"I dream of the oracle bones used by my ancestors to

foretell the future, of a small drum, and also of animals—
their eyes full of suffering."

To be honest, I don't know what Jim was thinking and
dreaming during the 125 years we were together on the
raft—from 1835 to 1960, although it seems now to have been
no time at all. I can't read minds, and Jim, by nature shy and
reserved, would not have shared his innermost life with me.
Some things I have to imagine, else there will be no story.
And if I have not been entirely truthful, it is not with any
intent to deceive. Mark Twain passed his book off as if I had
written it myself. I've told you before that it was none of
my doing. Frankly, I resent the words he put in my mouth.
If Jim were here, I'm sure he'd say as much. I'm not out to
correct Twain's mistakes; he's famous and has every right to
them. I want only the chance to tell the story in my own way
while I'm aboveground and in my right mind.

What was I thinking then?

God knows. Probably about the river: its bottom, bends,
shoals, reefs, and snags. It always fascinated me. When Pap
was sober, he would take me down to the mudflats, where
we'd do a little fishing. He liked to eat river carp. Before his
hands shook from liquor, Pap could scale and skin a carp faster
than any other man I know. I can see him now, against the
sinking river light, his bare arms glittering with pink scales.

My mother? Never knew her. You can say that my youth
was spoiled by men. I mean, I never knew the gentleness of
women, which might have smoothed and civilized me. The
Widow Douglas thought too much about the next life to be
of any use to a boy in this one. Miss Watson was a backbit-
ing screech owl of a woman without a charitable bone in her
body. She was as stern and unbending as a corset and had a

face like a broadax. In Hannibal, when I recommended killing her to Tom, I wasn't fooling.

I ought to mention the dead man Jim and I fished up from the river, north of Memphis. From his striped overalls and cap and the coal dust ingrained in his hands, his cheeks, in the loose folds of his bristly neck, he gave every appearance of being a locomotive engineer. But the wonder of it was how he'd come to be adrift in the main channel of the Mississippi. We had no answer, and never did discover anything to account for the incongruity. The night after we'd fished him up, I heard a locomotive beating its way downriver toward our raft—its cyclopean headlight looming in the dark. I put the blanket over my head and prayed like mad. It was only a lantern belonging to a towboat or a barge, but I couldn't shake my expectations of being sunk by a runaway train. You can't always be testing reality. Try, and progress will be slow and halting, like a man's on snowshoes crossing a snow bridge flung over a bottomless crevasse. You have to step out and hope the snow isn't rotten. I have always believed in recklessness and the amplitude of time, which are the creed and virtues of any boy.

After our encounter with the celestial railroad engineer, I took an interest in the deceptive appearance of reality, debating it with Jim while we meandered southerly in what must have been almost a state of suspended animation. My capacity for abstruse thought was becoming sly and subtle, like a seducer worming his way into a woman's boudoir.

"Do eels have souls?" I remember having put that question to Jim, as he brought one up from the depths, where, presumably, it had lived in contentment, maybe even joy, regardless of its lowly, uncharismatic appearance.

"If men have souls, then I do not see why an eel shouldn't," he replied with his usual sagacity.

But I thought he was being evasive, and said as much.

"Not at all," he said. "I'm inclined to give life in all its forms the benefit of the doubt."

"I doubt men have souls," I said, wanting to goad him.

"You're a skeptic, Huck, and you'll be the worse off for it if ever you grow up."

Of course, the argument probably went more like this:

Me: "Do eels have souls, Jim?"

Jim: "Don't know. Maybe."

Me: "What about human beings?"

Jim: "Good Book says so."

Me: "Good Book mention anything about eels?"

Jim: "No, only serpents."

Me: "Eel's a kind of serpent."

Jim: "Then it don't have a soul."

Speaking of appearances, I would like my future readers to know that the picture of Jim and me that Thomas Hart Benton painted on the wall of the Missouri state capitol bears not the slightest resemblance to either one of us. I look like a scrawny old man miniaturized, and Jim, like a muscle-bound grotesque escaped from a road gang. I've never been satisfied with any representation of myself and have seen only one picture of Jim that did him justice. I don't know why this should be, unless it is evidence of a nearly universal prejudice against us, instigated by Sunday school superintendents, Republicans, and bigots.

Time passed, but slowly as we moved toward the future, with what must have been antiquity at our backs. We would feel it suddenly like a cold draft upon the heart, making us shiver in fear. The past had vanished, but it still had power to influence us, while the momentary present engaged us in its toils. We were being carried onward into a space not yet woven on time's loom. There was nothing to be known—not even indirectly, the way unseen magnolia trees are known by the heady odor of their white blossoms. The future is said to be unborn. But how, then, do you explain the bottle of patent medicine we took from the water below Memphis, manufactured in Natchez in 1925? The empty bottle had floated impossibly *upriver,* bringing with it a future, assembled out of particles of nothing into a town.

"How could it happen, Jim?" I asked, mystified after he'd finished reading me the milky blue bottle. He was not an illiterate, having been taught to read by Miss Watson, who liked to "show him off" to company.

"Now and then, time must flow backward," he said.

"But the bottle rode upriver *against* the current!" I nearly shouted in my perplexity.

"Then the river must be like a Möbius strip."

Jim didn't know a damn thing about Möbius or his strip, although he was still alive at the time of its discovery. I'm only amusing myself. Anachronism is a storyteller's prerogative. But I know this much: We must head always toward the future. At least on a raft.

Then why, you ask, am I writing this book, which is a return to a dubious past?

What else can a man do who has used up his future? And if I should die before finishing this—what will happen to the boy and the black man on their raft?

EVERY THIRD DAY, I LET JIM BE CAPTAIN of the raft. I was captain more often than he because I took pleasure in it, not because I considered Jim incompetent. His pleasure was to take inventory of the valuables stolen from Miss Watson's and Judge Thatcher's houses. We had between us a mother-of-pearl opera glass; a phenakistoscope, with which we watched a Scotsman jig, a circus girl jump, and a bass fiddler fiddle; a barometer that neither rose nor fell but always stayed the same; an ivory-handled revolver without bullets; a bottle of cod-liver oil to pour down the throats of our enemies; *The Pilgrim's Progress* to read to our enemies as a punishment; two tobacco pipes, one corncob and one briar wood; a jar of navy plug tobacco; an onyx letter opener; a splinter that had entered Judge Thatcher's left foot in 1802 and emerged twenty years later to the day from his right foot; a stovepipe hat; a file in case Jim was ever chained up again; a petrified frog once belonging to Tom (the same frog Jim had seen Marie Laveau resurrect); a darning egg; a viola whose bow Tom had broken playing Robin Hood; Aunt Polly's christening spoon; a marlinspike; a frock coat; fire tongs; a cast-iron dog; the jug of rye whiskey; a box of locofoco friction matches; sealing wax; and a bar of Belgian soap in the shape of a hot-air balloon.

Jim liked to make up stories about the valuables: how they might behave if they could talk or how we might make outlandish use of them, such as steering the raft by whatever way the darning egg rolled, in order to avoid snags and wrecks, or sawing on the viola strings with the petrified frog. He thought this might raise a chorus of the dead and cause the varmints inside our clothes to jump overboard. He liked to tell me about the creation of the world from a handful of mud and thorns, about the moon's whispering secrets all night to the sea, the noise of stars, the drowned who coursed forever through the river's veins, a woman who ate her children, and the sad wedding of a weeping willow to a locust tree. Jim's themes tended toward sadness, which must come naturally to a man bereft of nearly everything.

Once, Jim shocked me by putting on a frock coat and a stovepipe hat (belonging to the judge), and with his hand gripping the sternpost as if it were a podium, he recited from memory Lincoln's Gettysburg Address. He would never say how he had come by the text, not even when I dosed him with rye whiskey to make him talkative. While Jim was no teetotaler, he couldn't handle liquor and would fall asleep before he could be coaxed into revelation.

"Do you think God made us all equal, Jim?" I asked when he had recovered his wits and the power of speech.

"Yes, Huck," he said simply, so that I was ashamed to think otherwise.

When John Wilkes Booth shot and killed Old Abe, Jim was inconsolable for days afterward, weeping and gnashing his teeth and jabbing at his leg with the marlinspike, until I feared he might throw himself overboard or at the very least lose his mind. I didn't know what I would do with a deranged black man on such a small raft. I thought of putting him ashore but couldn't bring myself to abandon him. I would sooner have set a Christian in a coliseum rampant with starved lions. Jim was my friend, and if grief turned him into a raving lunatic, then so be it.

We'd found the patent-medicine bottle in the fall of 1862, below Memphis. We floated down to Vicksburg, a distance of 180 river miles, in about one hundred days, arriving in the middle of the Union siege of that Mississippi town, on June 21, 1863. We'd made unusually good time for a raft steeped in legend, a speed Jim attributed to the overriding effect of "historical urgency." (Did Jim say that, or did I read it somewhere much later, after I had embarked on a serious study of time travel, commencing with Minkowski's *Space and Time*, which I didn't understand?)

Listen: Every author wants to write at least one time-travel novel in his or her life. If I failed to produce mine, it was not for lack of trying. I would lose myself in the bewildering complexities of the subject. After a while, I didn't know whether I was coming or going.

There was one other valuable, which I forgot to mention: a fragment of a meteorite that had fallen on the shore of Bull Shoals Lake, where Judge Thatcher had gone fishing for walleye. I have wondered, often in the years since our journey, if the "thunderstone," as Jim liked to call it, did not possess otherworldly properties. Jim would hold it to his ear as you might a conch to overhear the roar of a distant sea. He claimed he heard planets hissing down the black jetties of space, whales breaching tropical seas, an unknown music called jazz, and a prophecy of a second Flood.

The past is vivid. Don't you find it so? It's like watching a movie in Technicolor while the present, in which I am engulfed, is black and white and fading before my very eyes. A specialist in mental disintegration once wrote that mine was an extreme case of arrested development. Jim knew better when he said my boyish heart had been flummoxed by time and my brain soused by too much Mississippi River water.

AT VICKSBURG, WE LEFT THE RAFT for the first time since the winter of 1850. We could go no farther, because of Pemberton's cannonading from the bluffs overlooking the river and Grant's bombardment of the beleaguered town from the opposite bank. Outwardly, Jim and I had not changed. How our thoughts and tempers may have been altered by experience, I cannot guess. We had seen death pass by us on the river, but death had been ample in Hannibal, too. In those days, the mortuary parlor was not the exclusive precinct of the recently departed. Death was present in houses and on the streets. More than once, Tom and I had stumbled onto corpses while hunting river rats or searching the rank mud for pirate treasure. The Mississippi was a river of the dead as familiar to us as Lethe or Styx to the ancient Greeks, and occasionally it would deliver up from its abundance the well-washed bodies of the murdered and the drowned.

Jim and I hid the raft in a bayou and waited for the town to fall, which it did to hunger, dysentery, and malaria as much as to the ceaseless shelling by Union artillery and gunboats. The Confederates surrendered on the Fourth of July, 1863, and Jim and I wandered the ruined town and the "prairie-dog village" dug out of the yellow-clay hills above it. We marveled at earthen living rooms like caves domesticated by fancy carpets, beds and other furniture, with slaves to wait on tables, though their masters, after a forty-eight-day siege, had little to eat except their own shoes. Jim and I didn't think much about it, not being hungry ourselves. Besides our seemingly inexhaustible provisions, the Mississippi was generous with its fish. If Jesus had been in Vicksburg then—which he most certainly wasn't—he would have had more than three little fishes with which to work his miracle. My God, but the river was rich, unlike now, when we've sown the waters with poison and brought forth deformity and death unimaginable in the days of our youth. As I recall, Jim and I were never thirsty, either. We had aboard the raft a jug as miraculous as Cana's, which was filled always with sweet water. It was wonderful drizzled into rye whiskey.

The slaves looked at us with mistrust and, I thought, resentment.

"Because you seem to them a freeman," I said to Jim in explanation.

"Because for you, this is just scenery," said Jim. (Or maybe I read it in his eyes.)

He may have been right to think I made a cartoon out of suffering. He understood people better than I. Pain had made him sensitive; loneliness (he was lonely even when in company), alert to the slightest motions of the hearts of others. I wouldn't say Jim was a better man than I. To ennoble is to diminish by robbing people of their complexity, their completeness, of their humanity, which is always clouded by what gets stirred up at the bottom. Jim was only sometimes brave, sometimes good, and sometimes wise. The same can be said for most of us. And Jim never got the chance to flower or to fall.

That afternoon while the Army of the Tennessee was celebrating victory and Independence Day both, a photographer—one of Matthew Brady's—asked to take Jim's picture. I was annoyed that he did not consider me an interesting subject for posterity. For a reason I could not explain, I longed to have myself copied onto a glass-plate negative. To have my light stored away—carried in his lumbering darkroom up north, as if I wanted to resist a destiny already shaped for me, like an inheritance too onerous to accept. In that brief moment in which I sought to burn my image onto the negative, directly, without the intermediary of a lens, I matched my will against a stronger one, and failed.

"Step away, boy," the photographer ordered from inside the camera's black drape.

"Why not me?" I wanted to ask. "Why *them* and not me?" I gazed at a sullen heap of dead men, whom a variety of cruel deaths had made anonymous. I'd watched him take satisfaction in photographing them. They had no more interest for the eye than sacks of feed, although, in their perfect stillness, they had been accommodating subjects during the long exposure when they gave up the remnant particles of light. They would go underground in total darkness. But I knew the cameras that harvested in the sorrowful aftermath of that most uncivil strife were greedy for what still moved, as well as for what would never move again.

Then why not Huck?

"Clear out of the way!" he shouted at me, so that his camera might devour Jim alone.

I backed into the shadow of one of the white tents that dotted the hills like new lambs among the red placentas announcing their recent arrival. But here the scene was other than pastoral, and men leaned against rifles instead of shepherds' crooks. Inside the tent, I felt myself swallowed by silence. When my eyes adjusted to the dark, I saw around me, neatly laid out, a row of dead Union soldiers waiting to be collected . . . to be sent on. I rifled their pockets.

Later, when we were back on the raft, drifting south toward Natchez, I showed Jim what I'd taken to be added to the valuables: a pocketknife, a buckeye nut believed to strengthen virility, a signal mirror, chewing tobacco, a black-bound testament, a bundle of letters tied with a ribbon, a rosary, a photograph of a bride and a groom glaring in mutual accusation, a hank of chestnut-colored hair, a woman's ivory comb, a jaw harp, and a heavy key such as might have locked its owner for all eternity inside his sepulchre.

"It's wrong to rob the dead, Huck," Jim said softly. "But I suppose you had no choice. It's your nature, which was given to you. You're too weak to fight against its demands. You are like a fish hauled up out of the life you had believed to be your own."

"Do you believe in free will, Jim?"

"Is there a more ridiculous question to ask a slave?" he said, laughing.

And for a moment, I hated him.

BELOW NATCHEZ, AT RED RIVER LANDING, the Mississippi divides for the space of a small island near the middle of the river. As we swept toward it, we were hailed by a soldier who, along with his captive, had waded onto the islet's gravel beach from a sandbar where their skiff had run aground. The other man was Choctaw and looked as if, in better days, he might have been a chief or a shaman. He had remnants of what must have been a lordly dignity, although it was worn to rags by misery and sorrow. I didn't admire him for his suffering or for the obvious contempt with which he viewed his captor. If anything, I felt resentment toward him, which I didn't bother to understand. The day was hot, the yellow beach stifling. Unlike the soldier, who had rightly found himself shade, the Choctaw stood in the sun, as though it were only another insult to be borne.

"I should have taken the ferry, up above the reach," said the soldier, cursing his misfortune, which he attributed to the entire race of red men. "I lost the oar halfway across and nearly drowned myself in the goddamned river. Lucky for me, the boat ran up on the bar."

I could see that Jim was hesitating to take them aboard, in case they should be struck dead as soon as they touched the raft. He had speculated that the raft was a charmed space where we were kept unspoiled and unchanged, like fresh meat in an icehouse. But the raft could have the opposite effect on anybody else. I whispered to him from behind my hand that he should chance it. Frankly, I always did have a scientific inclination and thought the experiment worth the risk. Jim agreed, but I noticed that he took the soldier aboard first. I thought it was natural for Jim to favor the Indian, since they were both members of a despised race. The soldier got aboard with no harm coming to him, and the Indian followed wordlessly.

"I'm taking this old bag of bones back across the river to Indian Territory," said the soldier, letting river water run out of his boots. "Son of a bitch up and left without permission so that he could die in his ancestral homeland. Not that he would have gotten it. These good-for-nothings think they can lie down and expire anyplace they feel like. He claimed a railroad track ran across his tribal burial ground, and he had made himself a little place to rot, in plain sight of a train crammed full of congressmen. They were going to visit some Civil War battlefield or other, as if there wasn't one they could have paced closer to Washington. Self-righteous pissants raised a holy stink when they saw the chief. They didn't think a dying Indian, or even a dead one, added much to the scenery. This here Hiawatha is about as picturesque as mattress ticking left out in the rain. We'd just as soon have shot him and tossed his heathen bones into a sinkhole, but the bastards said they couldn't allow such infamy, not in the year of our Lord 1873. So I was ordered to take 'Cochise' back to his reservation—at the army's expense and my own considerable inconvenience."

The soldier glared at the Indian, whose eyes remained unwaveringly on his, registering in their dark depths nothing I knew how to read.

"I suppose I should thank you boys for stopping for me."

Jim spoke of providence and the sparrow as he swept the long oar back and forth in the heavy current; the soldier, of the pleasures of drink, beseeching us with greedy eyes to give him some of our whiskey. I spoke of the river's difficult navigation; and the Indian, of nothing at all.

In those days, I didn't much care for Indians. Injun Joe had colored my opinion of them, so that I believed they were, one and all, no better than cutthroats and drunken renegades. But when the old man slipped over the side of the raft and, having made himself a quiet little hole, sank down under the water, I thought a Christian and a gentleman could not have died more politely and more conveniently. I was feeling so favorably disposed toward him (I never did learn his name—Christian or otherwise) that I said not a word to the others until we'd crossed to the Mississippi's western bank.

I was tempted to return to the island. I liked how the water seemed to shape itself around it and wondered if a life there might not shape itself around me, granting me rest from our hectic journeying toward an end that had not yet announced itself. Neither Jim nor I had given any thought to a destination, trusting ourselves to the river—its will and deeper knowledge.

I did not know what I wanted. Now, at a moment distressingly near my last, I'm not sure I ever knew—not even when I'd gotten my hands on what passes for the world's exuberant bounty. Many years after I'd left the raft, I realized most of the dreams of a river rowdy, of a sneaking and thieving no-account boy. I had money, cars, women, a home not far from the ocean. Tom said that what a boy wanted was glory. I never heard him say what it was a man wanted. Not glory, surely. Maybe not even adventure, for glory and adventure stale. Love? Having known it only once, I'm not the best judge. Jim and I—maybe all we wanted was to fall, not from any height, but as a bird does, scudding headlong above the river in defiance of gravity, hoping to be saved from the terrible effort of resolve. I told you what Jim and I wanted was freedom, but I'm not certain anymore if we did. It's hard to live a purposeful life.

You say, this is no way to tell a story. That I've been merely threading one incident after another on a string of recollection and conjecture. Maybe so. But I don't know any other way.

Later, when we were once again on our own, I asked Jim to cast the bones concerning my future. He did.

"What do you see, Jim?"

"You will live long," he said, studying the augury, "but not happily."

And then he cast them for himself.

"What do you see, Jim?"

He shrugged and said, "Neither happily nor long."

I was sorry about that.

I've neglected to describe the beauties of the way. Let me do so now: The river was wide and brown. Where I had seen the water close over the old man's head, a cloud of midges wavered. The shore on either side heaved up into wooded hills whose trees shook and swelled in the wind that was corrugating the surface of the river and dispersing the midges before the trout could rise to them. (Thus are we cheated of our rightful expectations.) A shadow swung out suddenly like an enormous hinge, darkening the hills and also our raft. Our sweat-dampened shirts chilled us, and we shivered as though we held in our hands a warrant for our own deaths.

"Passenger pigeons," said Jim.

"Look at them!" I said in admiration, as anyone does who looks on immensity.

They were countless as stars, as grains of dust, as the dead lying underground or underwater. Birds in their millions, sweeping overhead like a dark aerial river. They moved as one bird, as if at the behest of a common intelligence. I thought to myself there would never be so many again. Jim scried their future in a crystal ball that had belonged to Marie Laveau, which all this time he had kept secret from me. I did not ask how he'd come to have it, whether she had made him a present of it or he'd stolen it because of a passionate, overmastering desire to see what is hidden from us.

"On September first, 1914, the last passenger pigeon left on earth will die in the Cincinnati Zoo," he said, wrapping the crystal in a piece of black cloth. "Her name will be Martha, named for the first First Lady."

"How can that be, Jim?"

"I see it and much else besides: the end of many, many species. The last of the elephants will die in chains," he said, and I knew he was thinking, too, of his own kind.

In 2034, during a boat show, I would visit the Cincinnati Zoo. There were no animals, only plasma screens, each showing a video of the poor beast that had once occupied the cage. The videos played in endless loops while zoo visitors tossed peanuts into the otherwise clean cages, in homage to what was irretrievably lost or as a ritual whose object was forgotten. I don't recall having seen a memorial to Martha. I do recall having seen in the capital a heroic statue in bronze of General Grant on his horse Cincinnati, whose genus, *Equus,* has very nearly followed so many others into extinction. I didn't give a damn, but now that I, too, have an end in sight, I feel sentimental toward all who are fated to disappear. Like tumbled columns, the wreckage of time is submerged in the river at its end—choked with the silt of hours beyond reckoning, compounded of blood, bone, gold, rust, and ashes. Jim and I shuttled toward the Gulf on time's vast loom—one year yielding to the next in a continuous stream whose noise was like rain or like the wind in Wyoming, which is said never to cease.

On the heights above Fort Adams, where the treaty had been signed expelling the Choctaw from their aboriginal homeland, a flaming cross was decorating the night sky. I thought it was a pretty sight. I wondered if I would see the old man again who'd killed himself in order to save time or trouble or else to rush into the land of the dead, which would—he believed in his bones—give him ease. If I were to come upon him standing ghostly on the river that had enfolded him, his eyes disks of sky overcast by clouds, would he have something to say to me, and would I him?

AT BATON ROUGE, WE ENTERED the twentieth century. We did so by night, like thieves stealing into a house we would ransack for unimaginable treasures and horrors. We knew nothing of what lay ahead on that river in space and in time. Not even Jim's prophetic gifts could enlighten us about the future's somber recesses, other than we would die in it. But we were entranced as anyone would be who sees for the first time a town made incandescent by Mr. Edison's lightbulb. At first, we thought the cause of our astonishment must be a myriad of candles or oil lamps strung among trees for some grand civic occasion. We had been born, remember, at the beginning of the nineteenth century, when the infant science of electricity produced little other than parlor tricks, and we had been well insulated from progress of most every sort on the raft.

"Looks to me like sparks blown up a chimney," I said. "Or else shooting stars laid thickly on the hills." I was an almost mythological boy who might have been expected to have a poetic streak. "Only it ain't. What is it, Jim?"

Jim said nothing, but I could tell he was becoming unsettled.

"What's wrong?"

"I don't know, Huck. But I have a bad feeling all of a sudden."

"But it looks *swell*!" I said, falling into the vernacular, which is to proper speech what mud is to a shoe shine. (I can't explain why my life should have been tainted by the character Mark Twain made of me. I've never forgiven him.)

"If you were to see a fire burning way off in the distance, you'd think it looked swell, too—even if it was somebody's house ablaze."

Jim was deep, as I've said on more than one occasion. But at the moment, his depth was that of someone who had sounded to the bottom of despondency. Yes, it had a bottom. Jim suffered much, but he did not seek, like some others, to make his life more tragic than he could bear. Or I could stand to listen to.

"We ought to investigate," I said, hearing in those words

the voice of Tom Sawyer, whom I had nearly forgotten during the years since we left Plum Point. "We could work our way up the cove and slip into town. Streets are likely to be empty this late."

Tom would have suggested a lark: minor vandalism of public property, a skirmish, a small robbery, bullying a defenseless boy, or a visit to a whorehouse, where he would hop straight out of bed and then out the window, without paying. (Women. Did we miss them? I was thirteen. Jim mourned his lost wife and children. Sexual desire was not part of our journey.)

Jim would not agree, no matter how I declared my wish to discover the nature of the light—unnatural in its cast and stillness; there was a small wind that night that would have set ordinary flames shivering or scattered the will-o'-the-wisps you sometimes see in marshes. No, these town lights were unmoving, and so was Jim in his refusal to go ashore. In the end, I had to respect his conviction that the lights—at first so astonishing in their novelty—did not bode well for two travelers in flight from their origins. I guessed that the town was under a curse, unless it was only Jim and I who were. Whatever uneasiness he felt about this place, at this time, soon jumped from his mind to my own, like a flea from one dog to another; and now I wanted also to be gone.

"We should get to Mexico," I said, having understood that America was dangerous.

Jim smiled at me as you would a child who has just said something wise. I was, remember, a child and I spake as one, while Jim was foolish only occasionally, like anyone who is mostly wise. For the first time since leaving Hannibal, I was afraid. I wished Tom could be with me, but the wish was momentary; for I knew—despite the namelessness of my dread—that not even the indomitable Tom Sawyer could prevail against it.

Jim and I were no longer aimless, although it could be argued that we were never so, having borrowed, unconsciously, the river's own ineluctable end: steadfastly south to the broad Delta and to the Gulf and from there to the world's far ends in space and also in time. I think now that we had been all along at the service of time, whose perfect materialization in history was the Mississippi, the great river, the father of waters. For good or ill, like it or not, it colored our thoughts and shaped our consciousness to its own unfathomable purpose.

"We should go," Jim repeated as he worked with his muscular arms the raft's long sweep until the current had caught us up.

WE HAD GONE ONLY A LITTLE WAY SOUTH of Baton Rouge when a steam launch came alongside the raft and a Western Union boy shouted, "If you're Huck Finn, as I suppose, and you want to see Tom Sawyer before he departs this world for the next, then you'd better hurry."

Suspicious of chicanery, Jim tried his best to dissuade me, grasping my wrist; but I shook off his hand and went aboard the launch. Several minutes later, I was deposited on the quay and directed to the place where my old friend lay dying.

I had no difficulty in finding the house, because of the electric lights that shone down upon the streets and from the homes of the well-to-do. Apparently, Tom was not one of them; he had fetched up in a small and shabby room of a dilapidated boardinghouse, like a piece of driftwood brought by the tide (his tide, the last but one, which would, at the moment of his death, carry him out onto the limitless ocean beyond the reach of history). The world had turned gaily for Tom Sawyer, though not for me; and shortly, it would turn for him no more. (And me? I had no idea of what lay around the bend any more than a fly does—nervously pacing a windowsill as winter's imminent death chills the sash.)

I took my friend's hand and wondered at its dryness, the wrinkled skin, fingernails long and broken, and at how a ring hung loosely on one finger. I brought the candle that burned with a meager flame on the bedside table nearer to Tom's face and saw—with a shock of surprise and disgust—that my friend was an old man. I did a quick calculation in my mind and realized that Tom Sawyer had used up nearly eighty years and would have no others to call his own. I closed my eyes and saw again the reckless, scheming boy who'd set Hannibal on its ear and, much later, the naval ensign aboard the Confederate warship *General Sumter*. I shook off the vision, which frightened me for a reason I almost understood—shook it off with a violent movement of my head and allowed the light to swell against the darkness, until it splashed the wall behind poor Tom's pillow and fell over the sheet shrouding his ruined frame. Then it was Tom's turn to open his eyes, and, having done so, his look registered a dismay and confusion the equal of my own.

"Huck?" he said weakly, so that I was forced to lean over him. When I did, I started at the smell.

"Tom," I said, and then said again, stupidly: "Tom. It's your Huckleberry come off the river to give you a send-off."

"I was dreaming of you," he said, and he seemed to come alive for an instant as he told me his dream: "We were back in Hannibal, out behind Miss Watson's house, and we had stuck Jim's hat on the branch of a tree. Remember how we persuaded him that witches had taken him all over creation while he was asleep?"

I nodded gravely, aware that Tom was about to be ushered into eternity, or extinction. You can't help feeling solemn in the presence of a dying man. I've known people to be boisterous around a corpse—I've seen the Hannibal constable summoned to a wake for a disturbance of the peace—but bearing witness to the approach of death tends to dampen even the most exuberant spirits.

"I knew you'd come to see me off," he said. "I sensed you in my dream, out there on the river."

For a second time, I nodded, having known stranger things than this in my lifetime. If Jim and I partook of the supernatural, I reasoned, then why not Tom Sawyer, who was more advanced in age and intellect than Jim and me put together? Looking back now from the vantage of my seniority (waiting for my own tide to go out, and with it me), I can't be sure the Western Union boy was of this world or some other. I wouldn't put it past Tom to have summoned him telepathically, in dots and dashes, if he was keen to have me escort him to the gate of eternity. As for the steam launch, it could readily have been of otherworldly origin: Ghost ships are familiar to anyone who has been to sea or even, like me, on a river as extraordinary as the Mississippi.

"Isn't Jim with you?" asked Tom, attempting to see past me into the shadowy recesses of his narrowing room.

"I ate him. Don't you remember?"

He gave a feeble laugh and said, "That was nothing but a hunk of fatback! You could fool those Johnny Reb sailors, but not Tom Sawyer. Pretty piece of legerdemain, though, Huck. My hat was off to you."

I was shocked to hear Tom confess so blithely to a serious dereliction of his duty as an officer.

"I left him on the raft," I said. "He's scared to come ashore because of the lights in the town. He took them for a bad omen."

"I'd like to have seen Jim," he said peevishly.

I couldn't guess why he missed Jim, whom he'd tormented in his childish humor, unless it was to ask for his forgiveness. But I wasn't much interested in Tom's mental workings, which could scarcely have been in order. I've since regretted the lack of curiosity, because of my own guilt in the matter of Jim.

Why?

I mistreated him. Not in the ordinary way of a bully or an ignorant white child lording it over a black man. That's not it, although I did behave sometimes as if he were inferior. I had the faults of my time and race. But I wrong Jim by reconstructing him in these pages. I've done to him what Twain did to me because I need Jim with me once again and cannot resurrect him any other way. Memory holds nothing in its sieve, except rubbish we clutch until the last hour, mistaking it for the truth, the facts, the real McCoy. I need Jim to make me real.

Tom shut his eyes and died without another word. I thought it a shame that he went before he could tell me if he saw anyone coming for him in the dark. I'd always imagined that someone would come, stealthily, even if all that could be seen of him were his shoes stepping in and out of a circle of lantern light, like a town watchman.

I looked through the dresser drawers to see if there was anything worth taking. I knew Tom would not begrudge me. None of the clothes fit, of course; and I had no use for a hairbrush nested with Tom's silver, a razor bearing Tom's stubble caked in dried lather, or a celluloid collar yellowed with Tom's sweat. But I liked the title of the book he'd been reading and took it with me: *The Time Machine,* by Mr. H. G. Wells. How very like Tom Sawyer to own such a tale of outlandish adventure! I realized when I was back on the raft that he had borrowed it from the Baton Rouge Public Library. I'm ashamed to say, it is long overdue. I've read the story many times since then and never fail to picture the Time Traveler as Tom himself, how he looked on the skiff, coming toward me from the *General Sumter.*

Yes, I'd been taught to read haltingly, in Hannibal by Miss Watson and the Widow Douglas as part of their campaign to civilize me.

I thought the book was a sign—not a bad omen, but a harbinger of good fortune; that it was a guarantee of safe conduct through the streets of Baton Rouge, which Tom had consecrated by having lived there and having also died there (which the more powerful juju, I could not know). My ideas were hazy and unformed about the meaning of Jim's and my journey downriver, but I guessed it had something to do with time travel. If not, why was Tom an old man while I was still a boy?

What year was it?

Nineteen hundred and three. April. The sixteenth day of April, in the year 1903. What day could have been more auspicious? The beginning of spring, of new life, the dawn of a new century. A new age. Charmed! And I supposed that the enchanted life Jim and I had on the raft was joined by a benevolent hand to the place where Tom and I met for the last time. I sensed (a raw boy could not have articulated it) that I stood at the convergence of two currents, two electrified rails—two "mystic chords of memory," as Mr. Lincoln said—and the rare, scarcely possible occasion of their meeting would protect Jim and me. I nearly called to Jim in my mind, with the intention of urging him telepathically to join me in a send-off Tom missed by too promptly dying. I felt he was owed an incomparable escapade, a grand bust-up, a rambunctious carouse. I wanted to run outside, into the streets of Baton Rouge, and commit high jinks and devilry in honor of our friendship. I was young, remember. My imagination was of a heroic cast and did not yet encompass low boozing and sex. I went through Tom's pockets but discovered nothing except an ancient letter from Becky Thatcher, a yellowed and brittle greeting from Jeff Davis, and some silver money—none of which had any value for me. (We had no use for money in those days. God Almighty, I'd whistle a different tune once I was off the river for good and understood that it is the universal balm and nothing whatsoever can be done without it!) I arranged Tom's hands as I had seen people do in Hannibal and pulled the sheet over his face. Then I snuffed out the candle, closed the door, tiptoed down three flights of stairs, and stepped out into the street with a sense of ecstatic relief that I had the power in me to escape the gravity of the deathbed. I was already forgetting Tom—so dismal is the idea of oblivion, so strong the attraction of life, even for someone like me who has kept his distance from it.

Darkness reigned, but not oppressively. The stars seemed hospitable fires in the April night, the moon smiled like a simpleton, and people milled noisily in streets made cheerful by electric light. I walked slowly toward the river, reluctant to enter the blacked-out stage of our little raft. I was sick to death of loneliness—of the absurdity of our journey.

I felt like Hamlet when he was delivering his "To be, or not to be" soliloquy, which I'd heard the Duke rehearse years and years before. I cursed myself for a fool because I hadn't sense enough to turn back when I could. I was homesick for dry land and an ordinary life where a boy can be counted on to grow up and die, which is the natural way of things. Maybe I was feeling no more than the restlessness of youth, which would will itself into adult life if it were able. Whatever the cause, I felt discouraged and forlorn. I put off returning to the raft awhile; I went to find myself some cheerful noise and light and people, no matter that I was already tending toward misanthropy. I clutched Wells's book for courage, while I walked streets made dangerous by my friend's death.

What else?

I rode a trolley up and down the bluffs, exhilarated by the luxury of horseless travel inside a conveyance illuminated by the same electric light that made the place a fairy town. I had no money, as I said; but I was used to getting inside circuses, magic-lantern shows, lectures on the pygmies, and other public entertainments without a nickel to my name.

On one street, people were jostling at the door of a building that had been converted from a grocer's store into a nickelodeon. I had no idea what a nickelodeon might be, but I was attracted by the bustle and laughter, which defeated solemnity and, with it, death. I slipped inside, as though I had no more substance than a shadow. Maybe I was one; maybe I could've strolled, brazen and unseen, through the streets, sat inside the trolley car while it lurched uphill and down again, and walked into the nickelodeon without taking pains to make myself inconspicuous. Maybe on that night in Baton Rouge, I was invisible to everyone but Tom, whose eyes were fixed on ghosts. In my life, I've often had the sensation that I was unnoticed to an unnatural degree; that I made no impression on others' optic or auditory nerves. Then in sudden terror, I'd act in an outrageous manner to make myself apparent. I was like a clean windowpane, unregarded until you accidentally shatter it.

Death had no dominion over me once the moving picture had begun. It routed the darkness, overthrew the gloom of melancholy. It astonished me as nothing before or since has done. *A Trip to the Moon*. The spaceship of the astronomers, their landing on the moon and battle with the Selenites, their escape back to earth, the rocket's sinking to the bottom of the ocean among strange yet familiar fish . . . The people who saw it with me that night were struck dumb with wonder. How much more must a boy born three-quarters of a century earlier have been? I never forgot it. *A Trip to the Moon*—by Georges Méliès; I suddenly remember the magician's name!—and *The Time Machine* have been for me bulwarks against the night. Not an April night in 1903, but those at the terrible end of days—without light, without a kind voice, without courage. The moving picture stopped, but the illusion of fantastic life continued awhile. I walked to the river and boarded the raft because it could not have been otherwise for Huck Finn.

I TOLD JIM THAT TOM SAWYER WAS DEAD, and he was sorry only as someone can be who has lost, beyond all hope of rescue, a portion of the past—that is to say, a vital piece of himself. I told him about the moving picture, and the idea fascinated him. Like a Hindu, he believed in the deceptive appearance of things: that the world is a thin film of light and shadows. What might be on the other side of that film, Jim didn't say. Maybe nothing. From what I've come to know of life, probably nothing.

"What should we do now, Jim?" I asked while he untied the line from a cypress tree leaning over the shallows.

My question was meaningless. We were in the current, which was a kind of intelligence: It knew the river's course and purpose; and even if the atoms of water enfolding us had not yet flowed into the Gulf, the current itself already knew the river's destination, though perhaps not its final end. We were held in the mind of the river, like a thought. The Mississippi knew what we would do next, notwithstanding the things that kept us busy: seamanly duties essential for life aboard a raft but, in the grand scheme, inconsequential. We were part of the Mississippi's design and had been since our departure and, if Jim were right, long before that. Jim believed in destiny, which is why, I suppose, he did not bother to answer my question.

When the sun rose, we had covered only a few miles of water since Baton Rouge, but we had left 1903 far behind us. Time seemed more than ever to lengthen the farther we got from the river's source. Years and years slowly passed—1910, 1911, 1912, 1913, 1914, '15, '16, '17, '18, 1919—and we felt only lethargy, a slight boredom, which we dispelled with songs, tall tales, fishing, and trailing our hands in the water, like two girls taking the sun. The sun was out more often than not, or so it seemed to me. Later, as I made the final passage alone, the sky would be black—or maybe it was only my own thoughts that were so.

Have you considered what this story might mean, or are you taking dictation with no other thought than the payment you'll receive when I have in my hands the transcript of this—what would you call it? An American picaresque?

A chimera spawned by an old man's grotesque imagination? And will anyone care? I wish I had Jim here to sound! He understood things better than I: the river, life, our helplessness, our desire—the human wish to be elsewhere and not alone. To be *un*alone, unlike me with no company but a hired amanuensis. I spent a long time in the world but never possessed the knowledge of men and women. Not even with her . . . Maybe the fault lay in my most unusual childhood. If it was unusual. Maybe at its heart—beyond the particulars of shape and circumstance—it was simply a childhood. If that is the truth, why have I failed myself? Unless we all do, but with the grace and courage not to grumble.

Below Plaquemine, there was at that time a mangrove swamp overgrown with cottonwood. Encouraged by its desolate appearance, Jim and I tied up there in order to stretch our legs. As we picked our way into the swamp to conceal ourselves, we heard a cornet playing a music unlike any other we had known. Its novelty drew us farther on into the swamp. How do I explain jazz (for so it was) and the effect it produces when hearing it for the first time? I can't, except to say it held in its volley of sound a mixture of melancholy and exuberance that thrilled. To listen to it was to be cast down and uplifted, at once. To be dizzied by emotions that, I suspect, were more available to Jim at that moment in our history than to me. That description of jazz is as wide of the mark as a greeting card verse is of a passionate truth. But I doubt I can get nearer. Maybe you can't with words. Mine anyway. Poets might, but their lines would only approximate the music's. Go listen to King Oliver or Louis Armstrong play their cornets—then you'll have an idea of what Jim and I felt among the tangled cottonwoods, but only an idea.

Shortly, we came upon a black man resting on a stump,

his horn flashing like a heliograph in whatever light managed to fall from the shifting upper branches of the trees. In the stillness of his deep concentration and in the way the dark green shadows commingled with his own native darkness, he resembled a cemetery monument. A dry stick cracked under my foot, and he promptly turned to me with a fearful look until he saw Jim.

"What's that you're playing, mister?" I said.

"Why, that's 'St. Louis Blues' by W. C. Handy. Haven't you boys ever heard jazz before?"

"No sir," I said. "We've been on the river for quite a spell."

"Jazz music's up and down the river," he said. "I was playing cornet with some black boys on the *Natchez* when the Dixie Shines came aboard at Donaldsonville. White boys don't like mixing with coloreds—never mind we swing way better than they do. Last night, them sons of bitches set me down on this island, with nothing except my horn to keep me company."

"Are you a runaway?" Jim asked, assessing the older man with a narrow look.

"Runaway? Oh, you mean like a slave."

Jim nodded.

"Ain't you boys ever heard of the Civil War?"

"We stopped at Vicksburg to see it," I said casually, pleased by the effect I produced.

The man now eyed Jim and me with mistrust.

"What are you boys?" he asked.

"Just two people floating down the Mississippi on a raft," I said.

"From where?"

"Hannibal."

"From when?"

"Eighteen hundred and thirty-five," I said. "What year is it now?"

"Nineteen nineteen."

The news surprised neither Jim nor me. We'd already guessed we were traveling in all the dimensions known to humankind at that moment in its history. I'd been reading *The Time Machine* to Jim, and given our experiences of the past eighty-four years, we deduced that our raft was a time machine of sorts, well suited to a pair of country boys growing up on the river. We had a hard time, however, convincing the man—whose name was Henry Wilson—that we were otherwise than two disreputable con men. When we'd finally overcome his disbelief, Henry showed an eminently practical cast of mind by suggesting we take him with us into the future—at least until we reached a point in time when we might expect human nature to have improved. Jim was skeptical concerning a future golden age, but he agreed. I hesitated because of the cramped conditions aboard the raft. But in the end, Henry Wilson joined us in our southerly journey.

"So, there are no more slaves?" Jim asked him.

"No. The war and Mr. Lincoln's proclamation put an end to that evil."

"And you're a freeman?"

"In some places more than in others," Henry said wryly.

"Meaning what?"

"In the South especially, a black man must tread lightly if he don't want to get himself lynched."

"What's *lynched*?"

"Hung up by the neck from some tree branch or lamppost."

Jim and Henry spent long hours in conversation, heads

bent together, while I made a show—in jealous annoyance—of steering the raft with immense effort and concentration. My exertions were a pretense; the river had a mind of its own, expressed by the current, which was sometimes headlong and at other times contrary. Jim and Henry traded thoughts, the river kept its secrets, and I leaned against the sternpost like a man up against a taproom's bar without a worthwhile thought in his head.

As we slipped effortlessly downriver, scarcely aware of the Mississippi's hold on us, Henry told Jim about a war he'd fought in France, at Château-Thierry and at Belleau Wood. He'd been a soldier of the 369th Harlem Hellfighters, a black regiment raised in New York City for the defense of civilization. Henry's Great War reminded me a little of what Jim and I had seen in the aftermath of the siege of Vicksburg. But mostly, I could form no clear picture of his travail from the words he used to describe it.

He spoke to Jim about garlands of twisted wire hung with dead men and also with living ones who screamed out their agonies until friend or foe could stand it no longer and—in pity or in sudden anger born of an overmastering irritation—shot them, allowing silence momentarily to pour its balm over the devastated ground. Henry spoke about cages of fire falling from the night sky, about poison gas clouds that smelled like geraniums, mown hay, apples, or almonds. He spoke, too, about winter—its gray snows growing minutely on the barrels of machine guns and cannon, on the broken boots, iron helmets, and great coats of the unharvested dead. It might have been a foreign tongue in which he spoke. I understood very little of what Henry said.

You're right: Henry would never have said this, would not have uttered such high-flown crap. A lyrical turn of phrase—no matter how impassioned—cannot capture cruelty, terror, waste, stupidity, and death. Only plainest speech is apt for the occasion of so much misery. What he might have said, as he leaned against the forward post in his baggy corduroy suit, was this:

"I sat in the rain or snow or stench, in a shitty ditch that was muddy, freezing, or choked with dust, according to the time of year. I pissed myself in fear, played cards or had fistfights out of boredom; I got drunk when I could and prayed to go home. I got no medals or kisses on the cheeks from French generals. Instead, I got lice, crabs—caught the clap once—and spent two weeks in the hospital for trench foot. Lucky for me, I lost only one toe, the little one, which I wasn't using anyway."

Maybe. Maybe not. I never went to war, although I did go to a prison, of sorts. I've been scared many times, but not as Henry must have been—or Jim would be, before his journey's end. But you make do with what you're given, and I've spent a good many years learning to write fine-sounding sentences so that I can hide behind them. It's the way of the hermit crab, with nothing to recommend it but the pretty shell it annexes for its own. Henry scared me—worse; he'd given me the taste of bitterness that comes when you realize the world is irredeemably evil. I wanted him off the raft, as you would someone with a fever, a sickness you're afraid to catch.

Buzz, buzz, buzz! They spent their time, whispering together like two spinsters—like Miss Watson and the Widow Douglas, whose meanness and piety were unsurpassed. Like flies crawling on the inside of a window, wanting to get out. I got so I hated the sight of their woolly heads. What in hell did they find to talk about all those years?

The years passed: 1920, 1921, 1922, 1923, 1924, '25, '26, '27, '28, '29, 1930. And in all that time, Henry aged no more than Jim or I, which was not at all.

"We're far enough into the future for you to get off," I said to Henry when Edgard, Louisiana, came into view around a bend. Jean Lafitte had favored the town's rum and women with his swashbuckling presence. I doubted Henry would be welcomed with an equal warmth.

Jim took me aside and said we should wait a few more years; he didn't think we'd given *Homo sapiens* nearly long enough to improve its low character. He thought the job of civilizing human beings was far too big to be accomplished in only a single decade.

"Give him another ten years," Jim said. "What's ten more years to us who never alter in time or feel the least inconvenienced by its passing?"

His concern for Henry hardened my heart. I pulled at the sweep oar until the raft scraped up onto a gravel beach, and then nodded to Henry, who understood and got off with his cornet. For a moment, I feared Jim would get off, too; but he remained aboard, although he turned his back on me— whether in disapprobation or disgust, I don't know. I pushed the raft off the gravel into the river, and we were once again in the current. We spoke not a word while the river reasserted its influence. I looked over my shoulder at Henry, who shrank until there was nothing left of him but the sunlight on his horn. The sun vanished in clouds, perfecting Henry's obliteration. The world seemed to have hushed, with only the "St. Louis Blues" to disturb the mournful silence. And when we had put the town behind us, Henry's music was drowned in the noise of water and of the wind that blew with the force of history at our backs.

JIM WOULD NOT SPEAK TO ME, and the years passed in silence. I hated him and might have tried to knock him overboard if it were not for the feeling that my destiny was entangled in his. (I believed at the time that I had a destiny, separate and apart from what the river willed.) Could I go on without Jim? What would it mean for my life, for his to end? That he could have considered himself bound up in Henry Wilson's fate didn't occur to me—or if it did, I put it out of my mind as a complication beyond its power to unravel. Time slowed as though it meant to stop. I worried what it might mean to me if it did. Would the river, raft, and we two seize up, like a watch in whose works a bit of grit or rust has lodged? Jim did not speak to me, nor I to him. I longed for a scrap of conversation or even a bone of contention we could have gnawed aloud. I don't mind silence so long as it is companionable. Standing at the sweep oar, I looked at Jim's back as he sat well forward on the raft. When our positions were reversed, I looked at the river and its shores.

Let me describe once again the beauties of the way: There were swans toward shore that knotted behind them long threads of brown water; and herons standing on one leg, necks preening in the light or elongating suddenly to spear small fish flashing in the shallows; and pelicans straining at the oars of their wings; and geese that hurtled down from the upper air, flailing as they skidded to a stop on the face of the water. There were animals onshore drinking from the river and others on the headlands and in the hills. The trees on the hills and in the valleys and pastures beyond them were green or the color of old gold or, farther to the east, white— in their seasons. I knew how the land lay on either side of the great river that divided it. And I had it on good faith that the earth was rich and yielded ample harvests unless it was a time of drought or scorching heat or annihilating rains. But they, also, had their places in the shaping of the people's character. So, too, the western desert and the northern plains and the smoking cities of the East. The river was not so wide as it was up above, but deeper—its depths communicating to me a knowledge of shoals and reefs and of other things hidden from view that give us fear and also hope: the one, that we will founder and drown; the other, that we will avoid—by luck or providence—the snares and continue on our way into a future that may be better than the past.

"He may have played his cornet in the town hall," I said to Jim at last to break the silence.

He turned to me and said, "Yes, he may have taken the train to New York and played with Louis Armstrong and Fletcher Henderson or gone to Chicago to play with Jelly Roll Morton and King Oliver." (The men's names meant nothing to me, since, unlike Jim, I hadn't "been to school" with Henry Wilson during his years on the raft.)

I've never known whether Jim was serious or sarcastic at that moment. In any case, the ice between us had broken, and we talked while we floated so very slowly downriver. But it was never the same again, and our talk was not easy or pleasant anymore. Time drained away like sand in an hourglass: a figure of speech that makes up for its unoriginality by its exactitude.

The years rolled on: 1940, 1941, 1942—there was another war, but we didn't feel it—1945, 1950—and there was yet another war—1954, '55, '56, '57, '58, '59. . . .

In 1960, Jim decided to leave the raft for good. We had been on the river for one hundred and twenty-five years.

WE PUT IN AT WAGGAMAN, on the west bank of the Mississippi. Jim took his pipe and several plugs of tobacco, the darning egg, the stovepipe hat, and *The Pilgrim's Progress*. We shook hands formally and gravely. He left the raft. I watched him until he disappeared down a side street. I sat for a long time, wondering how it would be to go on without him. Twice, I attempted to gather myself together and push out onto the river, but I couldn't. I smoked a pipe, drank a little whiskey, and wondered why Jim had taken the darning egg and not his petrified frog. In the end, I followed him into town.

My feelings at that instant—what I can recall of them from this remove in time and space—were complicated. I was bothered that I had come to hate him, bothered even more that I had loved him. I'm not sure that I regarded him then as a man. Not entirely. That broad view of humanity was alien to a mind that had been formed haphazardly, like a shack put together out of old lumber, warped and ill-used. There was about me then a makeshift quality. My nature was rough-hewn. I was cruel and envious because I was often afraid. I regretted I had not been more open with Jim. We'd wasted much time when we might have understood what was happening on the raft while we closed in on the river's end, which was not to be the journey's end, as I learned later. No, it was not even the end for Jim. I went on with him—we went on together—for a long time afterward.

Jim stopped at a house and knocked at the door. I watched him fumble off his hat when a bedraggled young woman stepped onto the porch. I was hiding in the bushes, and I heard him ask if there was any little job he could do.

He needed money for a bus ticket, he said. He wanted to go to New York. I wished then that I had taken the coins from Tom Sawyer's pocket so that I might give them to Jim. The woman looked at him with scorn and with something I couldn't interpret.

"I got an old chifforobe needs busting up for kindling," she said.

"I'd be pleased to do that for you, ma'am."

"You can call me Mayella," she said, giving him that disquieting look again.

Sensing in her what I could not, Jim began to back up on the porch. But the woman insisted and took his arm and dragged him into the house. Shortly after, I saw him carry the chifforobe into the yard and chop it up with an ax while Mayella stood and watched.

Finished his work, Jim asked politely to be paid, but the girl wasn't ready to see him leave.

"Come into the house," she said, "and I'll give you a cool lemonade to drink. You look all hot and sweaty."

I could see Jim wanted to light out of there. But he was hesitating. Maybe because of his desire to go to New York City, maybe because of something that had to do with Henry Wilson—I don't know. Jim went inside, and in what seemed like the next instant, he flew out the door again, without his stovepipe hat. He hurried down the street. I followed him to the bus depot and hid behind a pile of mail sacks, where I could see him waiting on the "colored only" side of the station.

One bus departed for St. Louis, another for Chicago. But before the New York City bus could leave, a pickup truck, half-eaten by rust, stopped with a screech of worn brakes in a cloud of dust and black exhaust. Three men in greasy overalls and sweat-stained hats jumped out, grabbed Jim, and threw him into the back of the truck. Behind the steering wheel, a man smoked a cigarette with grim determination; beside him sat Mayella, chewing on her hair. A second truck appeared and then a third—all three filled with the same overalls, hats, and bristling cheeks and chins. They formed a convoy and drove out a dirt road into a mangrove swamp by the river. I'd climbed into the back of the third truck. A man gave me an ax handle and told me to beat the n——— with it when we stopped. I held it; it was a kind of ticket to the proceedings. I watched Jim sitting in the truck ahead of us, his feet dangling from the tailgate as if he were going to a picnic. He didn't struggle; he never said a word. I hoped he didn't see me.

What is it you want to know? Did I want to see Jim lynched? Is that what you think?

No, I did not. I don't know what I wanted as the truck bounced and bottomed out on the ruts, but it wasn't that. I held the ax handle. I was scared. I prayed they'd just give Jim a beating and let him go. I held the ax handle, but I had no intention of hitting Jim with it. Can't you understand what goes through a boy's head at a time like this? I was scared, and I wanted to be sick. The men with me were like drunks: eyes glazed, mouths open in an ugly leer, their lips white and gummy with saliva, strings of spit stretching like rubber bands when they opened their mouths to curse the n———, to scream how they would kill the n———. Jesus Christ, I wished I were back on the raft with Jim, or without him! I held the ax handle and felt tears start in my eyes and wiped them in shame with the dirty back of my hand. I think I said to the man next to me that I wanted to get off the truck. But the truck didn't slow until the road came to an end, and then all three trucks stopped. I think I jumped out and crawled inside a clump of cottonwood bushes and lay on my belly and shook. I think that's what I was doing when they pulled Jim down from the back of the truck and put the rope around his neck and hoisted him up on a branch. I don't remember if I looked. All I remember is the noise the rope made while it swung slowly back and forth with Jim's deadweight at the end of it. Then it began to rain. They didn't leave him dangling in the tree. They made a joke about sending a package to New Orleans. They cut Jim down and threw him into the river, with a length of rope still around his neck. The way they laughed, it must have been funny.

I waited in the cottonwoods until night came, and then I stumbled through the brush to the river, where I made my way along the shoreline to the raft. I rowed out to the middle of the river and tried not to think of Jim anymore.

I SURRENDERED MYSELF TO THE RIVER, its secret purposes. But the river said nothing, except in the way of water: liquid syllables unintelligible to my ordinary mind. Jim might have understood, but not I. Which is not to say that I, like any other boy, did not hear voices in the babble. But they were only those spoken by a childish imagination: the bloodthirsty speech of pirates, the boastfulness of riverboat gamblers, the bravado of soldiers on their way west to subdue the Indians. I knew none of it was real. I was tormented by loneliness.

The beauties on the way. There was none to be had; nothing to excite the senses or busy the mind with the effort of recognition, nothing to uplift the heart or lighten the

gloom, nothing to resist the pull of memory and the gnaw-
ing of remorse.

Was I sorry?

No, yes, no—what could a boy have done against a
dozen ruffians with ax handles, knives, lead pipes, and a
rope that knotted readily around Jim's neck, as if the destiny of hemp were to lynch black men? What could I have
done other than I did, which was to shut my eyes, to wait
for the dark, to get away, to get back aboard the raft and
wash my soiled pants in the river?

Courage?

Courage didn't come into it. I was obedient to my body,
whose every cell screamed self-preservation.

Time must have finally stopped or come as near to stopping as the laws governing physical existence allow. I saw
an old movie made from an H. G. Wells story about an
insignificant man whom the gods give superhuman abilities.
He stops the earth from turning, and everything—houses,
cities, people—flies off into space. I must've been afraid
of something like that happening, although I wonder if I
even knew that the earth turned. I was a fairly ignorant boy,
remember; and such a fact would not have been common
knowledge among children of the 1830s. What did, in fact,
occur was—how do I describe it? Think of how it is when
the balance between light and dark tips, when there is more
night than day, when light seems to drain out of things and
things begin to fade, growing more and more indistinct.
I seemed to be drifting—no, not drifting: stalled. No, not
even stalled, for one can sense in that word the potential to
move. But I sensed no such thing.

What did I sense?

I sensed murkiness, gloom, faint noise, a smell like ozone,

the taste of a nine-volt battery when you lick the terminals, the sound you sometimes hear when you put your ear to a railroad track, a grayness, a sullenness, the smell of old cellars, a lassitude, a numbness, a noise of a solitary airplane high above the earth, turbidity, odor of dust, of earth, of nothing at all, the taste of stale water, stale air, smell of old books, of must, tar, blood, burning oil. All of it. None of it. I was alone. That much I knew if I knew nothing else. The river was gone, or I was steeped in it so completely that I could no longer recognize it, any more than one who is sleeping can recognize sleep. Not that I was asleep. While my sensations were barely intelligible, I did feel; I was aware of tastes and odors, no matter that they seemed to float free of any source. They were a sensory reality proving to me that I was not dreaming and could not have been asleep.

Decades passed unknown to me: 1960, 1970, 1980, 1990. . . . I was aware of little more than those raw, confused sensations. Things did happen in the world, of course: wars, the collapse of regimes and economies, revolutions, riots, assassinations, epidemics, more wars, mass slaughters, catastrophes, murders, extinctions, space flights, moon landings, the discovery of exotic particles, dark matter and energy, black holes, the age and origin of the universe, inventions, elations, horrors—fear happened and death and love also happened, but not for me. I knew the history of the era, only because I read about it much later. But by that time, I was living among men and women who had no memories, who were indifferent to public events in the wider world; like them, I was improvising from day to day, like a man without attachments or a future. I had forgotten the river. I don't know whether or not the river had forgotten me.

The second millennium arrived without my noticing.

Time weighed on me hardly at all. I was not in it—or if I was, I was like the raft, lightly held by the river, without a keel to bury me in its element. Like the raft, I displaced very little; and that is the secret to existing apart from time. To be weightless is to be outside time, the heaviest element. I sensed my future was drawing near—that is, the point where I would reenter the world. I believed it would be Mexico, that old dream. Had Jim ever talked to me of Mexico? I can't remember.

And what about Jim? I can't help wondering what his body might have done to the river that upheld me. Did it change it a little as tea leaves do water? Did it alter it profoundly, contributing Jim's atoms to the river's own? Was I with Jim while I passed blindly down an unused passage of time: a back channel long ago closed as unnavigable, a worm hole that would shortly deliver me into Mexico? I wish I could recall whether Jim had said anything about Mexico. I could make something up, I suppose. I've done so often enough. But what good would it do?

The years flowed into one another: 2001, 2002, 2003, 2004. . . . The river reasserted itself, although not entirely. It materialized as if it were emerging from a fog. As if the world strained toward recognition and revelation where nothing is recognized or revealed. Yes, that is what it was like: An ordinary fog—wet, bluish gray, and pervasive—replaced the tumult of sensations that had been the world for me, as it is for a blind person. No matter I could see only a very short distance at any compass point; fog was a common occurrence on the river. I had dealt with it many times before this. I imagined that, when the fog lifted, I would see New Orleans.

Once more, I could feel the raft moving, and with it me.

Time quickened, and my body registered a slight pressure: what a barometer might feel in the moving column of mercury. I felt heavier; my body began again the ancient struggle with gravity. I was not yet completely in time, neither had I been returned, by motion, to the special time of myth, of the literary history in which I had been immersed . . . how long? Since 1835, when Jim and I had set out on the raft. Maybe longer. What do I remember of the thirteen years of childhood that had gone before the start of our journey? Light and a feeling of lightness, which are no more than vague recollections of childhood, summoned in old age.

What else?

A few vividly colored memories of having played by the Mississippi and in Hannibal's streets and alleys with Tom Sawyer and Becky Thatcher, of having tormented Jim, of having been afraid of Injun Joe, of having hated Miss Watson and the Widow Douglas. Of a circus, a minstrel show, a tent meeting. I'm infuriated by a boyhood that seems, even now, not to have belonged to me but, rather, to have been *written* for me; and I fear much of my adult life has been spent in a futile resistance to fate. Many times, I did bad things for no other reason than I believed I was acting contrary to what Presbyterians call "predestination." By whatever name, the notion upsets and revolts me. But maybe we live our lives in just that way. What about you? Nothing to say? You look half-asleep. I would send you home, but my story—the first part of it—is nearly finished.

The fog still had not lifted at New Orleans, but I could hear the city, its sounds coming as if from a long way off: noise of cars, trucks, buses, trains, and also ships of varied use and tonnage, blaring horns, tolling bells, the steam whistles of factories and the roar of airliners flying unseen high above me. I speak, of course, in hindsight; I was not yet of the world or in it. I couldn't know what the world had become in my absence. But in my heightened sensitivity, I also heard people at work, in love, in contention, at war, at their prayers, beseeching mercy, love, release from pain; heard people dying solitary deaths. In this, the world had not changed, nor will it ever.

You won't believe what I'm about to tell you: I saw Tom Sawyer and Jim, Henry Wilson and the old Choctaw Indian—as they were in life or as they are in death, I couldn't say. One by one, they appeared to me out of the fog. None had a word for me although I thought I saw Tom raise his hand to salute me, to wave good-bye, or to summon me. I don't know. What do we know? What can we tell or say about another? Jim wore the cut piece of rope like a necktie. Henry clutched his cornet. The Indian looked as if his eyes were gazing on the beyond.

Do I believe in ghosts?

Having been one myself, I do believe in them and in much else besides that is strange and doubtful.

Two thousand and five. August. The twenty-ninth day. Plaquemines Parish, Louisiana. At Venice, southernmost town on the Mississippi, called by some "the end of the world," I reentered the world and also time.

TIME BROKE OVER ME like an enormous wave, and I was overthrown by its weight and finality. (To admit time is to admit its end.) It staggered me, like an ox by the sledgehammer. I fell to my knees, but with no thought of praying; my fear was too immediate and electric, crowding out all other thoughts but it. Besides, I had not the habit of prayer and would rather have cursed God in stubborn contrariety because of Miss Watson's belief that a child could be made pious by the rod and cod-liver oil. She'd tried them on me often, and failed. Unless you were ever, even for a moment, outside time, you can't know what it means to be thrust into it. Maybe those who die and venture a little way toward the light or the final darkness, only to be pulled back once more into the body, know; maybe those under the influence of certain psychotropic drugs do. But I suspect you've experienced neither death nor a powerful hallucination. If you don't mind my saying so, you have the look of a cautious man who does not stray far from the polished rails of time.

All around me, while I clung to the sternpost, the winds roared. The sweep oar was gone, and soon the raft would be capsized by waves of water that the hurricane caused to accumulate into a mounting surge. Sky and river appeared a seamless gray, relieved by blackness. I had never known fear to equal this moment's, which increased with time's strengthening hold on me. My mind was emptied of everything save the danger, the cold misery of my sodden clothes, and the pain in one hand from desperately clutching the post. Had I been able to ask questions at that harrowing instant, I think it would have been these: What will it be like to drown *in time*? Will it be more painful than drowning in water when my lungs fill up? What organ does time—rushing in with the force of an arriving wave—swell and burst? I've since wondered at the tenacity of life: how it clings to the sternpost marking its outermost limit—to mortality's outpost, if you like—when, by opening a hand, we might end our fear and pain forever. (Unless Miss Watson and her hellfire sorority were right about the afterlife, though I can't believe those obnoxious souls could have been right about anything, except my own cussed and irremediable self.)

A noise was heard during the wind's bellowing, like splintering glass, as if I'd gone through a window separating the geometric certainty of rooms from the violent irregularities of the world outside them. A noise announcing—with a crash of falling millibars—that a hurricane whose name was Katrina had reached the point to which its forces had been straining: the saturation of matter by energy. Electrified, my hair stood up; the air crackled; the sternpost and the lean-to's frame (canvas torn away) trembled with blue and violet lights of St. Elmo's fire. The air grew thinner as its atoms rose, and the world would have yielded to the seduction of weightlessness, had gravity, momentarily weakened, not resumed, and with it time. Unused to it, I would have been crushed if the raft had not been overturned at that instant by the unpent surge. I was thrown into the river, which retained a measure of timelessness—or if not so absolute a quality, then a record of past ages held within its turbulence: moments of the history that had shaped it since leaving its source at Lake Itasca and its origin, as far as humankind is concerned, in the fourth millennium before the Common Era, when, in its fertile valleys, squash, goosefoot, marsh elder, and sunflowers were cultivated by indigenous peoples, whose later flowering included an old Choctaw Indian. If my mind had not been overwhelmed by terror, I might have thought him a fool to have gone peaceably to his death in this same river. (I take a different view of rivers than Heraclitus did.) But nothing crossed my mind while I struggled up from the river's black depths into the rain—saved, I have never doubted it—by the past, which has always been kinder to me than the present ever since I reentered time, off the western bank of the Mississippi, at Venice, on that catastrophic August Monday in 2005.

I've said before, how I resent the idea that a will alien to my own should be in control of my life: providence, fate, destiny—call it what you like. And something about that moment when there seemed no other possibility than death by drowning has always worried me. Strange, isn't it, that I would feel otherwise than jubilant thanksgiving for my rescue from drowning—by water? I continue, to this day, to be drowning in time and will do so until my last breath. Don't think I'm ungrateful to have escaped a painful death. But my escape weakened my faith in chance and the lucky accident. You see, I prefer to think that my fortunes and misfortunes are either of my own doing or else the result of a broken cog or gum in the works—a broken data chain or genetic sequence (to be modern)—rather than by design, God's or Mark Twain's. I ought to have drowned! There was no other reasonable outcome after being knocked from a raft into the water during a category-three hurricane. But I didn't drown, because at the very instant I reached the surface, a crate was waiting for me. And I heaved myself up on it.

Yes, I said "waiting," for so it seemed then and seems even now, seventy-two years after the fact. When I say "waiting," I'm not suggesting that the crate was motionless during the upheaval. It was moving downriver, like me. (It's more remarkable, by far, for two things in motion to intersect.) I was saved by the confluence of the crate and myself, and a moment later both were caught in the backwash of a sixteen-foot wave, transported onto land, and set down, with amazing delicacy, among the tombs and monuments of Venice's only cemetery. And yet I was not dead! The crate had entered the Mississippi at Minneapolis decades earlier (fallen from a pier or loosed into the water after a ship-wreck) and had made its long way downriver to Venice, with the intention of lending me its buoyancy. I might just as eas-ily say I'd been thrown into the river in order to give mean-ing to the "life" of that crate. See how absurd the notion of predestination is? Yet circumstantial evidence screams to me that it is so. The complicated machinery of fate was put in motion for my no-account self.

I slept in a narrow space between two gaudy sepulchres, sheltered from the brutality of the storm. The cemetery was a little above sea level, though not enough to allow for graves to be dug. The dead rested above ground, immured in brick and stone, as they must when buried near water. Whether from exhaustion or from the shock of having been expelled from childhood (how else explain so deep and unnatural a sleep?), I didn't wake until the storm had moved seventy-five miles northwesterly into New Orleans. I woke with a start and shivered as with cold, my pockets filled with crumbs of time like sand in those of a drowned man washed up on a beach. I was once again alive in the world, which I had not been all the long while I did not age or change.

When I was on the raft, I had moved from one incident to another. But they were not demarcated clearly the way they are in this memoir, which must seem to obey a chro-nology or it cannot be told. But those incidents—so col-orful in the telling—did not impress me at the time with their particularity, but instead were experienced—like the river down which I floated—as a steady lengthening from an increasingly far-off past. For a long while after making landfall, I felt my past tugging at me, like a fishing line that stretched back to Hannibal in the 1830s, its hook rankling at the corner of my mouth. Unlike a fish, I didn't resist—didn't seem to feel the present. I was immune to its contagion, and if I pictured a future, it was only a vestige of my old dream of Mexico, which I had not relinquished.

The rain stopped, and the charcoal clouds unraveled in the departing wind. Where all had been drowned by noise of wind and rain, the sound of the world at peace flooded back: gulls rowing the blue air from their inland retreat, the fitful breeze stirring the unfallen cypresses, and river water rattling over stones. It was as though the summer once again drew breath.

With a flat gray rock, I battered open the crate that had buoyed me to safety. Inside, I found clothes, shoes, socks—all of it made as if for me, so well did they fit. There was also a first edition of *The Adventures of Huckleberry Finn*, published, according to the colophon, in London by Chatto and Windus in December 1884. Despite an origin fairly remote in space and time, the book appeared to be newly printed and had suffered not at all by the crate's lengthy river journey. I opened to the first page and read there words pretending to be mine: *You don't know about me, without you have read a book by the name of "The Adventures of Tom Sawyer," but that ain't no matter. That book was made by Mr. Mark Twain, and he told the truth, mainly.* I read no farther and under no circumstances would I have turned to the last page.

Enraged, I threw the book into the river. I would have burned the damned thing had I a match, but the box of locofocos had been lost, together with everything else Jim and I had brought with us from Hannibal. Burning the book, I felt, would declare my outrage emphatically, might even remove it absolutely from existence, as if there'd never been a book by that title or an author by that name—so naïvely did I reason. But I had no match! I watched the book slowly turning in an eddy, its hard covers spread on top of the brown water like wings. I waited for it to sink, but the damned thing remained afloat and soon had escaped the gyre and was off downriver—a bird of evil omen. I threw stones at it, but my aim was poor; or else it was endowed with an intelligence native to books that eluded my fusillade or was under the protection of providence, that infernal engine, and could not, for reasons known to it, be sunk—at least not by a mere boy who only now understood the feebleness of his human presence in time. In a short while, the book was beyond the reach of my stones and of my influence—slipping toward the Gulf. Perhaps it would reach Mexico, I thought, when Jim and I had failed. I cursed it and Mark Twain both for their presumption. What did either know of my life's adventure or of Tom's? No more than I had known Jim's thoughts or might know those in the brain of a dog. I despised the book and its words, which had been set out like a trap to take my freedom. I promised myself I would act in a way to guarantee my self's independence. I couldn't have known that—twist and squirm as I might—my course was set. I'd be the man Huck Finn would most certainly have become in the age following the last sentence of Twain's book. At least for a while. Given the age, which was fallen and corrupt, and given the experiences—innocent and also sinister—that had shaped my character, I could be nothing else.

What did you say?

No, no, I did finally escape the life that had been given me to lead until its final agony or surprise. I'm changed—maybe not greatly changed, but enough. Enough to matter in the case of my life—the occasion of it. I swear I am!

What changed me?

The usual things. Love, if only in a small way. (You cannot

depend too much on love. It is something else than a means to your transformation. It's a selfish idea to believe otherwise.) Love changed me a little, and also the world did, as it can when it strikes fire against the mind's flint. And I was changed, too, by something that I will insist, always, was accidental: an instant of senselessness and absurdity when I fulfilled the river's purpose and my own.

PART TWO

August 29, 2005–September 11, 2005

NEVER GOT TO MEXICO, BUT MEXICO, as it turned out, came to me: a morsel of its fecundity, indifferent to our well-being, wrapped in plastic, with a street value well over $800,000. At the time, I had no knowledge of this brand of smuggling by water or of the vernacular favored by an outlaw economy flourishing in the twenty-first century. I was thirteen, remember. A boy who'd been floating through life—his life, at a safe distance from current events.

In the 1830s, I might have joined a band of roughnecks to smuggle Caribbean rum or slaves into the Missouri Territory. (The word *trafficking* was unknown.) I'd have done it for fun and so would Tom Sawyer; we were the product of our time and saw no harm in strong drink or in the ownership of other human beings. You'd be wrong to judge the boy I was then by the standards of the present age—and this you should know, too: I wasn't the innocent people have made me out to be. That's Twain's doing: His Huckleberry Finn might have had a kernel of goodness. People say so. But I'd have been embarrassed to think I had a spark of decency. No boy wants to be thought of as good. The world and especially girls find bad boys attractive. Don't they? Oh, it was a very long time ago, but I'm sure I was a devilish child, thoughtless, and casually cruel. A boy, as is often said with a smile, who liked to pull the wings off flies or hang up cats by their tails. Such a boy is hardly good and, in all likelihood, will turn out mean.

I don't wish to belabor this, but before we begin the

second part of my history, I want you, at least, to understand how it was for me when I got blown into time by
Katrina. Maybe I am trying to understand myself. Before
this, I've taken up such thoughts like a tangle of dirty
string; but I never tried to untangle it. Look, I'm just as
divided as the next one; but my case is unusual, except
among lunatics. Don't you think? God, I wish Jim were
here! He'd know what was troubling me. He was a slave,
and I tormented him and loved him. Jim was no fool. He
loved me, and I'm equally sure he hated me. That's what it
means to be human. I wonder if he hadn't been lynched,
what he would have become. The first black president of
the United States, perhaps. Let's leave it at this: I was no
better than any other boy and not so bad a man as I might
have been for the times. Think what you damn well please!

You can see for yourself I haven't long to live. Ha! I don't
hear you arguing the point. I am eighty-five years old, vari-
ous organs of mine are in revolt, and I am almost tired of
this life. I wonder what the next one will be like.

Yes, I believe in an afterlife—in dwelling, at least for a
while, in timelessness, which may not be the same thing as
eternity. With my history, how could I believe otherwise?

IF I FEARED THE CLOTHES, SHOES, AND SOCKS I'd found
in the crate because they might be part of an insidious
design whose purpose was my enslavement, I put them on
anyway. My pants were wet, my shirt a rag; the shoes had
gone overboard when the raft capsized. It may have been
August in Louisiana, but I shivered with cold. The hurricane had sown wreckage on the ground, dangerous for
even a boy used to going barefoot. I walked through the

remains of a cannery to the riverbank and headed toward the Gulf. I hadn't a destination in mind. I was looking for someone who might give me food and fresh water. I sensed that to walk northwesterly along the Great River Road to New Orleans was not for me: To return to a point in space I'd gone by on the raft would mean going back in time, impossible for someone no longer outside it.

Nothing moved except dirty wavelets of exhausted river water, a few listless birds, branches of the cypress trees, fitfully, and—strange and sad—two flat-bottomed rowboats on the flooded grass, which made me think of the Venice I'd seen in one of Judge Thatcher's books. But in these boats, no gondoliers sang barcaroles to lovers stunned by moonlight. I was alone with a graveyard of partially tumbled stones, a stove-in pier, dead fish on their way to corruption at my feet. I took a boat and, with a piece of board found in the flotsam to serve as rudder, pushed out onto the river and floated twenty miles to Port Eads, at the end of the Mississippi. Of that final leg of my journey on the father of waters, I remember how the river leafed greenly with fallen branches above its rushing mud, like Birnam Wood moving toward Dunsinane.

There was nothing magical about this brief trip downriver. I was finished with magic, and magic finished with me. I was alive and growing; I could feel my cells divide, my hair and nails minutely lengthen. I was acutely aware of the sensation of being alive in the world and in time—a novelty I experienced in a way no infant could. The feeling soon passed, and life became ordinary. The river pushed—or say, instead, the river upheld me while I steered, because I was in control. (I have to believe that this was so!) In time, I arrived at Port Eads, with its lighthouse and fishing camp, both of which had survived; and, just beyond the broken piers, the Gulf of Mexico shimmered like the dream it was.

THE CONNERY BROTHERS, EDGAR AND EDMUND, were cooking a chicken over a fire in an oil drum that had been cut in two when I walked out of the tall salt grass. Attracted by the smell, I was too hungry for caution. Time had restored to me the appetites, present or potential. Startled, Edmund drew a pistol from his belt and fired. I'd have been shot dead if Edgar hadn't knocked his brother's arm to spoil his aim. The bullet struck a mangrove tree. The report alarmed the birds, which rose up as one, like a congregation rising in unison at the sharp crack of kneeling benches striking the floor. (Have you never thought about the collective consciousness of gregarious things that fly, swim, or crawl?) I hadn't flinched. I stood my ground—a wild, grimy boy whose eyes, I was told later, looked overcast by a somber, unsettling emotion strange in a child. I think they were only wide and unfocused, as they will be when coming out of sunlight into gloom.

They did not know what to make of me. Edmund tucked his pistol into his belt and stared dumbly, the way one would at a monstrous thing, amphibious and scaled, that had crawled on all fours from the fetid mangrove swamp. I was a dirty, ragged boy. I listened to the swamp breathe and, sweeter, the Gulf seethe and settle. I wished Jim could see it, blue and vast. Neither of us had laid eyes, remember, on any water not bound by two mud flanks and brown with particles of dirt. Endued with sympathies his brother lacked, Edgar nodded for me to sit on a log near the burning drum.

"You look starved, boy," he said.

"I am, sir."

"We've got a chicken—the last one left at 'the end of the world.' Edmund pulled it out of a tree, where it'd gone to roost before the storm. A miracle chicken! Seemed a shame to kill it, but we're hungry."

"Not enough meat to split three ways," Edmund grumbled. He looked at me as you might at a rabid dog.

"Can't let the boy starve!" Edgar snapped.

I blessed him for his defense of helpless orphans and would have signed on, then and there, to any scheme he might propose, regardless of danger or legality. What did I know of either, really? In Hannibal, Tom and I had risked a beating for sneaking into a tent show or a steamboat minstrelsy. We'd pretended to be cutthroats and dreamed of glorious deaths, funerals, and resurrections. By an accidental escape from the universal fate of humankind, I'd been spared—provisionally—Tom's end and also that of Jim, who had grown a conscience and perished for it. My years had been charmed, but were no longer so.

With a brand-new barlow knife, Edgar cut off a chicken leg and set it on a plate for me.

"I'm afraid we've only beer to drink," he said.

I accepted the beer—the first I'd ever drunk—and would sing odes to hops, in my mind, forever afterward.

"He likes it, Edmund!" Edgar said, amused by my wrinkling nose.

Edmund was not amused. I knew he wished the bullet had planted itself in my chest instead of a tree trunk. Look, I'm only guessing at how this scene and dialogue went. It happened seventy-two years ago. I've got the mind of an old man who likes to remember what never happened and to forget what did. Don't think for a moment none of this is true! I swear it is. But seventy-some years is a long time, and I was a writer, of sorts, fond of embroidery.

I could not keep my eyes open, because of the beer and my exertions coming from Venice on the river and in the swamp. I shut my eyes and slept.

I OPENED MY EYES ON A PLANKED CEILING close overhead. By the swaying movement of the berth and by the creaking noise of straining planks and ropes, I knew I was on a boat tied up to a dock. I crawled from the berth and looked out a porthole onto a channel winding through a marsh of black mangrove shrubs and cordgrass. A reddish egret stood on one leg, making of its long neck an elegant S. I supposed the channel wound its way to the Gulf, which was hidden by the green marsh. The sky was low and lacked the crystalline purity lent by the departing storm. The humidity was increasing, and the air in the little cabin was close. I tried the door and was relieved to find it unlocked.

On waking, I was scared I'd been made a captive by the Connerys, although I felt the older brother, Edgar, was kindly disposed toward me. Edmund, I didn't trust and even feared, recalling his anger and impetuousness. I opened the door and stepped into a narrow passage, then climbed the companionway to the saloon, where I met James Toussaint, a black man from Trinidad. When he smiled, I noticed a front tooth clad in gold framing the white enamel with the cutout of a heart. He wore a gold-braided captain's hat bought, I learned later on, in a theatrical supply store. He was drinking rum from a halved coconut. Tom's aunt Polly would have called him—her tone an alloy of affection and disapproval—a "character." Had she been living still and aboard the boat, Miss Watson would have flown into a rage at the mere sight of him—wanting to pry the gold from his mouth, wash it out with soap, and purify his innards with castor oil. Or if she happened to be bilious, she'd demand Judge Thatcher hang him, without pausing to blow his patrician nose into his fine linen handkerchief, from Hannibal's ancient oak, which served frontier justice and the town as gallows.

"How're you doing?" asked Edgar, entering the saloon.

"I'm fine," I said, easing into a barrel chair opposite the black man with the fancy hat.

"You were out on your feet, friend," he said. "Edmund and I carried you aboard and put you to bed. I see you've met Jimbo."

"My name is James," the black man said, much annoyed. "James Touissant. Formerly of Port-au-Spain, Trinidad." He began what would have been a slovenly and ironic bow toward me if there had been no table and rum-filled coconut in the way. Foiled, he lifted his head and showed me his mouth's gold valentine.

"James is touchy about his dignity," Edgar said, saluting him. "And that's okay with us, because James is a first-class captain. We were lucky to get a man so at home in these waters."

"And what would you be called?" James said to me.

I would not be Huckleberry Finn, Huck Finn, or any other of Mark Twain's creatures. Just as I'd drowned his book, I would rename myself in order to begin life anew. Hesitating behind a feigned fit of coughing, during which Edgar brought me water, I hunted the air for a name and, seeing there the one carved above the black iron door of the sepulchre where I'd hidden from the storm, took it as my own.

"Albert Barthelemy."

"It's a pleasure to meet you, Albert," said James, raising a mermaid-topped swizzle stick as though it were an aspergillum poised to sprinkle me with a blessing.

"So, Al, what're you doing out here all by your lonesome?" Edgar asked.

And then and there, I created from whole cloth a story of my life. (It was not the first I had told and would not be the last.) I don't intend to retell it now, except for my recent bereavement.

"We were living in a shack by the river in Venice when the hurricane blew Pap, Ma, Uncle Jim, my brother Tom, my dog Duke, and me into the flood," I said. "Pap, who was a shrimper, got tangled in his nets and drowned. Twisted up in her nightdress, Ma followed him in death as she had in life, obediently. I managed to climb onto a crate the size and shape of a coffin. Meanwhile, Uncle Jim was trying to rescue Duke from a whirlpool, but before I knew it, both of them had drowned. I reached my hand out to Tom, but his mind seemed elsewhere; and in a minute, he was drowned, too, the light in his eyes put out forever. And there was nobody left in the river except me."

I was enjoying myself immensely while I spun the yarn. I've always taken pleasure in invention. Of Tom Sawyer's many and varied talents, the most admirable to me was his way with a story, which he could concoct, complicate, and elaborate with a facility and artfulness I consider nothing less than the stuff of genius. I paused a moment in the narration of my own fabrication, taking a drink of water—not because my throat or my imagination had gone dry, but for dramatic effect. My confidence in my ability to take up the thread, now that I had found it, was unshakable.

The storytelling impulse was unstoppable once it had seized and fired my brain. I've never identified its origin—whether the gift of some muse that might be a spirit residing in the ferment of barley and hops or else in a more radiant atmosphere such as Swedenborg or Blake imbibed. While I took another draft of water, I looked out over the rim of the glass at my audience: James sat on the sofa with the coconut at rest on his knee, the mermaid swizzle stick in his hand like a conductor's baton at the moment of a downbeat. Edgar leaned against the saloon bulkhead, hands in the pockets of his dungarees, his expression frozen midway between curiosity and pity. I had them in the palm of my hand, so to speak, and renewed my recitation.

"I rode the coffin—it seemed one to me after watching my family perish—downriver to the end of the world. On the way, the coffin bumped up against roofs and porches, barns and gazebos, Sunday schools and pianos, drowned pigs and cows—the whole mess of it moving toward the Gulf, like one of those Mexican parades where saints are carried through the streets by people dressed in black. It was a regular procession of last things, a flotilla of death. I lay on the coffin and waited to expire on its lid—struck by a floating tree, stabbed by a steeple or a weathervane, or smothered by an outhouse, its half-moon grinning at my corpse like a village idiot goggling at a passing hearse. I was ringed round by destruction: trees toppled; cars and pickup trucks flipped onto their backs like box turtles tormented by cruel boys; houses gone with the wind, their cast-iron bathtubs like something ancient and saurian muddling on clawed feet."

Did I use those words and speak in just that way while I told them my story?

Those words or others, in that way or in another. However it was said, I went on with glee.

"The river churned with mud. On its bank, mud lay thick and oozing, rank with rotting crabs, their insides torn out by rapacious gulls, cormorants, and brown pelicans. Had I slipped off the coffin lid and drowned, I knew they'd soon be banqueting on my guts. The coffin plunged and shook and swerved in the contrary currents and rapids. I held on for dear life and might have prayed if I had not been made to in the past by a good Christian woman, who liked to lay a white sliver of soap on my tongue, like a holy wafer. I gripped my coffin and cursed—words truer to my nature than prayer—and looked down into the tangled water, hoping to catch a last glimpse of my family or, at least, the dog."

My audience had increased by one: Edmund squatted in the saloon doorway, grinning at me while he twisted the point of his knife on his palm. He was a perfect specimen of Neanderthal man. His spite was universal. Not content with hating me, he despised fully grown *Homo sapiens* of either sex, as well as dogs, cats, insects, the fish he caught and savagely brained against the gunwale, even the squid and ballyhoo he used to catch them. He loved to test the temper of his knife on flesh—thawed or frozen. Flaying me would have been a pleasure.

Edmund was named for a villain. In fact, both brothers had been given names recalling the fraternal pair in *Lear*. Their parents must have been exceptionally droll, or vicious. To call one son after an infamous bastard and the other after a character famed for virtue is to predispose them to brotherly strife. The joke was diabolical, like that which Mark Twain had played on me, annexing my name for fiction and making it a hobble to keep me in character. The similarity of the brothers' given names made matters worse. To call themselves Ed resulted in misunderstandings, but Edgar and Edmund sounded ridiculously old-fashioned. Perhaps Mr. and Mrs. Connery—assuming their union had been sanctified—thought such highfalutin names would toughen their sons and make them mean enough to get on in the world. Or maybe they loved *King Lear*. I have, ever since the duke of Bridgewater introduced me to this and other works of the immortal bard when Jim and I were traveling together. (I'm not sure, now, whether that memory belongs to me or to the other Huck.)

"Horse feathers!" said Edmund, remarking on my story.

You don't believe he said "horse feathers."

Neither do I. Not such a piece of work as one who'd stab his brother in the back. All right, then: Let's settle the issue of verisimilitude before you take down another word. Edmund, Edgar, James, and most of the other men and many of the women I met during my days and nights as Albert Barthelemy were casual in their employment of obscenity. It was a spice to enliven conversation, a rude noise for the elimination of silences, a sign of bravado and stylishness. For most of my life in the twenty-first century, I was no better than anybody else. I said (let me say them once and be done with them) *shit, fuck, cunt, motherfucker, bitch, cocksucker,* in addition to lesser terms of opprobrium like *prick, twat, jerkoff, turd, dickhead,* and *douche bag.*

Years ago, I experienced a kind of—what? Beatitude, revelation? No, nothing so exalted. I don't want people to think I was abnormally good or virtuous, like those pious, hypocritical pismires Miss Watson and the Widow Douglas. (Goodness is a problem, isn't it? How are we to be good in this world, in this age, and not seem laughable and absurd?)

What has complicated matters is my questionable beginnings—and their remoteness from the present: Doubtless, I behaved according to the lights and customs of the time. But I could no more see the truth than Newton a boson or Hans Lippershey Uranus's moons.

I wish I could remember—truly—the life I led then: what I did and the actual words I said. Obscenity, for instance—profanity, as it was called. What dirty words did Tom and I say to provoke the sadistic spinsters to yank us by the ears to the kitchen sink and wash our mouths with soap? I'm not convinced that the choicest curses available to us then were *tarnation, cussed, bull, quim, blazes, bollocks,* and *lickfinger.* Can you imagine a sailor of the time drawing his knife on a mule skinner and muttering murderously, "I'm gonna cut off your bollocks, you cussed lickfinger!"? Do you believe Abe Lincoln, reared on the frontier, swore "blue blazes" at Mary Todd? In any case, how Tom and I cussed can never be known: The participants and witnesses are deceased, or soon to be. What Edmund probably said when I'd reached a stopping place in the story of my rescue was, "What a crock a shit!" And that, reader, is my sole concession to literary naturalism.

"Shut your damned mouth!" said Edgar, a rebuke endearing him all the more to me.

"Let Albert finish," said James, who would have been called, regrettably, by Deep South rednecks, a n———, not only in 1835 but also in 2005.

The villainous Edmund glared, clutched his knife, and went out on deck, silencing even the squabbling gulls.

"My brother's manners stink," Edgar said, nodding for me to continue.

"I did not know the color of the sky," I said solemnly.

"Eyes fixed on the water, I raced along, on top of my coffin, while the jetties narrowed and quickened the current. The river sounded like lard on a skittle or a sack of snakes. Just above Port Eads, the coffin snagged in branches of an uprooted swamp oak and slewed sideways against the current. It changed course as if I'd pulled hard on a sweep oar, jumped a low bank, and slipped into the flooded marsh. After a while, I came to rest in the high salt grass near the fishing camp. I lay, worn-out—brain reeling with what'd happened to me. Grief-stricken for my drowned folks, my brother Tom, Uncle Jim, and old Duke, I cried until I smelled your chicken cooking and came out of the swamp, hungry and generally miserable. The rest you know."

"And you've got no family living anywhere?" asked Edgar, his voice soft and whispery.

"None," I said, lowering my eyes from his—not in shame or embarrassment, mind you, but for effect. I'd learned the dramatic arts in company with the duke, who'd played Hamlet, Prince of Denmark, in London's Drury Lane Theatre. Or so our handbill claimed in boldfaced twenty-four-point Baskerville when we trod the boards in a hellhole of a town in Arkansas, whose name I don't recall.

"It's a crying shame!" said James, taking off his fancy cap like a man coming into a house where there'd been a death. I liked him for it, even if the occasion for his delicacy was a lie.

Did I mind telling so personal a lie?

Since I hadn't killed off anybody real in my imagination—no, I didn't mind at all.

"I'm an orphan," I said softly. If I'd had an onion, I would have oozed tears.

You disapprove. Well, you're wrong! I might not have been recently bereaved, but I was very much an orphan and alone. I hadn't many folks to call mine to begin with, except for Tom and Jim, after a fashion. I didn't even have a dog to lick my hand. And in all the wide world in the year 2005, I knew none and none knew me, but for these three men. Who wouldn't shed tears—genuine or false—if, like me, they had lost what little they had?

"James, a moment if you please?" said Edgar.

James nodded, emptied his coconut of rum, and followed Edgar out the saloon door and into the cockpit, where Edmund was savagely beheading a mangrove snapper with a bloody knife. James and Edgar stood with their backs to me, but I saw plainly how Edmund scowled. I wondered what they had in mind, without the least anxiety. I knew I'd be more than equal to their scheming. I was wonderfully sure of myself in those days, feeling, no doubt, a vestige of the mythic world in which lately I had traveled.

I turned the pages, idly, of a magazine devoted to the breasts of women and another showing men pulling great fish from the water by their gills. I'd have thumbed a magazine promising, on its cover, a body with the strength and endurance to wrestle alligators, subdue bears in hand-to-hand combat, and make women scream in ecstasy if James had not leaned in through the doorway and asked me to step outside. I put the magazine down and never did remember to open it again, though, like most thirteen-year-old boys, I was fascinated by alligators.

"Yes, sir?" I said, squinting in the sunlight glancing off the late-afternoon water.

"He's a well-behaved boy," James said approvingly.

"Yes, he is," Edgar agreed with a broad smile.

Edmund mutely scowled.

"Al—do you mind if I call you Al?" asked Edgar. I was

flattered by his deference. He could call me by any name he pleased so long as it wasn't Huck. "Seeing as how you're alone in the world . . ." he began; and then he hesitated, saying, "You are telling us the truth, aren't you, Al? There's nobody that will miss you?"

"Nobody at all, sir."

James picked at his tooth's golden valentine with the mermaid swizzle stick, and I thought, momentarily, of the overthrow of enchantment and the ruined world of myth.

"Then why don't you come with us?" Edgar suggested, looking at his brother, who growled a fierce assent.

My nose wrinkling, I sensed the possibility of an adventure that would impress even Tom Sawyer. Then I recalled that Tom was dead and a long time underground, and a tear coursed down my grimy cheek. The tear was genuine. Uncertain of themselves, the men shambled foolishly.

"Poor boy," said James.

"Pathetic," rumbled Edmund ambiguously.

Edgar put an arm around my shoulder. Affection such as this had never before been shown me—not even by Jim, who knew better than to touch anyone belonging to the white race, regardless of how dissolute. Soon, I was crying in earnest. Embarrassed, the men went inside the boat, leaving me the cockpit to wallow in. Thankfully, emotions Tom would have considered unbecoming were rare in me. I blew my nose nonchalantly into my hand, after the fashion of boys everywhere (and of professional men like baseball players, who find themselves marooned in a desert of grass without a hankie). After wiping my hand on the back of the transom door, I went into the cabin to see what would come next.

"Where're we going?" I asked, sliding behind the galley table, next to James.

He was poring over a nautical chart. I'd seen enough of them to know, in steamboat chart houses where Tom and I had crept in hopes of discovering the location of sunken ships that might contain treasure. We were always interested in enriching ourselves, although we never found anything more fabulous than arrowheads and the teeth of prehistoric sharks, dug from the mud below Hannibal.

"Across the Gulf to the east coast of Florida, then up the Inland Passage, across the C&D Canal to Delaware Bay, south around the Jersey capes to the Atlantic, then north to Atlantic City," said James, tracing the lengthy route with a scaly index finger. "Should take us twelve days, barring the unforeseen."

I must have looked either dazzled or baffled by the possibility of a second journey—a right smart pace in space, if brief in time. Edgar felt obliged to elaborate on James's sketchy itinerary.

"It's a fishing trip," he said. "You'll be our gaff man, mess boy, steward, and mate. What do you say, Al—sound like fun?"

It did sound like fun, but I wasn't sure I wanted to exchange a raft for a fifty-eight-foot twin-diesel fishing boat. If anybody deserved shore leave, after 170 years on the water, I did.

"We need to leave *now* if we want to make Gulfport before dark," said Edmund, reminding his brother of the urgency of their departure.

"What about it, Al? You want to come, or stay and wait for the Coast Guard to show up?"

I thought of spending the night alone in Port Eads, without fresh water or a chicken to be plucked from a tree. I looked at the saloon, with its upholstered chairs and sofa, at the galley, with its stove and a box from which Edmund had just taken a beer, beaded with condensation like a bottle of milk from the icehouse. I recalled the cabin where I'd wakened on a soft mattress and a pillow—the light from the porthole, stained green by cypress trees, falling on me like an insinuation of a world beyond worry and travail.

"They'll put you in the New Orleans Superdome with ten thousand other homeless people lined up for the toilets," Edgar said. "When they find out you've no family, they'll stick you in an orphanage. Not much fun there, my friend."

"Time to move!" Edmund barked.

"I'm afraid he's right," said James, folding up his chart. "We'll lose the tide and the light if we wait much longer. It's now or never, Mr. Albert."

All three turned their eyes on me. I was like a fish, free in its ignorance of the dragnet that shortly will begin to close on it, circumscribing its life with each haul on the line, till not even a sliver of freedom is possible. My instincts warned me to take my chances in the bayou, but the moment had already crystallized around the contrary decision, indifferent to my qualms. (All my life thereafter, at each crux, I would wonder just who or what threw its weight into the scales, deciding my next move.)

"I'll go," I said in a voice drained suddenly of possibility.

Did I regret my choice?

Yes, no, yes, no, catch a tiger by the toe. Think of any momentous decision in your own life. You have a wife, I know. Do you regret having married her? It doesn't matter whether you're happy at this moment or not; instant by instant, your mind wavers, unable to make itself up. Instant by instant, for as long as you both shall live, regret and contentment will be interchangeable terms in your life's balance sheet.

"I'll go," I said, this time with a greater show of enthusiasm. I did not want to go with them, and yet I did. Our fear of the future and our thrill before it are concurrent in us—even, I sometimes think, if the future can mean only death.

Edgar clapped me on the back; Edmund gazed inscrutably at me; James saluted with two fingers touching the garlanded visor of his cap before climbing the stairs to the bridge to wake the sleeping engines. Moments later, the boat lurched. Gravity and the heaviness of matter reinstated themselves. A boy who'd never been to school or watched a science documentary could not have articulated the physics. My back and buttocks pressed against the chair—a sensation to remind me of my place on earth, bound by iron physical law.

I remembered *The Time Machine* found by Tom Sawyer's deathbed. A slow reader, I'd never finished; and it had changed the terms of its existence to become a lump of papier-mâché or, reduced to its elements, a primal goo retaining not a word of its former self. No, I could be wrong. Whatever's left of the book may keep the memory of its vanished words. I would prefer to believe that things possess the power of recall, of recollection. That things are memoirs of the existences that once were theirs, if only we knew how to read them. This is what illuminates the merest stone or shell, arrowhead or shark's tooth. This is what can make mud shine. And Tom? And Jim? And me at the end of my time? Our bones, the carbon of their pulverized dust, will tell a story of our lives.

I sat in the companion's seat, next to James while he led the boat out from the bayou into the Gulf. Ahead, its water had turned golden like a molten ore poured down from the foundry of the sun. It slipped and rolled in shining disks, and white ibis, gulls, and albatross, come to rest or hunt, turned golden, too, like idols. Much later, in a travelogue, I would see a holy man walk down a stone ghat into the Ganges and sink to his chest into such a gold. The water, at this late-afternoon hour off the Mississippi coast, might have hidden in its depths the ancient water gods: Repun Kamui, Lir, Mazu, Vedenemo, Galene, Chalchiuht-licue, Kanaloa, Idliragijenget, Mizuchi, Tangaroa, Nammu, and Rán, who, in her nets, collected drowned men for the Norse. Of course, I knew nothing about the heathen deities—my religious education having been limited to what I saw enacted in Sunday school Nativity and Easter plays. Miss Watson would tempt me with cookies and doughnuts to spruce up and bruise my backside against a hard pew. But while James steered northeasterly for Gulfport, I felt what must have been reverence. Maybe an intimation from my own timeless days reached me while I sat on the bridge and stared at the transfigured water. Or I may have sensed the presence of gods with whom—unknown to me—I'd shared a mythic past.

You're right, it sounds far-fetched, even for me. Why don't we put it this way: Childhood had made me susceptible to evening's fugitive beauty. Those sensations of awesomeness—nettlesome and unfamiliar—must have scared me; I broke my spellbound stare and turned to James, like a boy throwing stones at a stained-glass window to prove himself a roughneck and a clod. No boy wants to be thought an angel!

"What's that sticking in your ears?" I asked, pointing to a Y-shaped wire disappearing into James's blue-denim shirt pocket. It was, I tell you, a diversion, nothing else: I didn't want to appear flummoxed in front of James.

"My iPod," he said, his hand beating time on the polished ball of the throttle. "It's music, man! Where've you been hiding, Mr. Albert? On Mars?"

If only he knew. I leaned toward him and heard a faint and distant singing, reminiscent of a wasp caught in a jar of marmalade. For all I knew of iPods, the sound really might have originated on Mars.

"That's 'Slave Driver' by my righteous man Bob Marley. Listen up, Mr. Albert," James said while he pushed one of the "buds" in my ear.

I listened without enthusiasm. I did not dislike what I heard; I was indifferent. My heart had moved too strongly toward a recognition of—how do I say it without sounding impossibly vain and pretentious? I guess I can't, and the reader, if I have one yet, must take me as I am: thoughtful. Call me a thoughtful man who wishes to make himself understood in matters closest to his soul and is in love with words.

So, my heart had transported me, while I watched the golden Gulf water slide and churn up ingots, toward a recognition of transcendence and eternity. Even a boy born on a mudflat can sense, sometimes, the weight of things and see, for a moment, what the moment holds. I had drifted into familiar waters—not that I'd been on the Gulf before. But a timeless feeling stirred me, produced by the light and a sweetness carried on a seaward breeze across Chandeleur Sound. Good Lord, what would Tom Sawyer say to hear such hogwash, such a load of bull? Don't misunderstand me: I did not yearn for my past life on the river. I was done with it. But in years to come, I'd grow nostalgic for it nonetheless.

The sun had nearly vanished behind me. The shadows

on the bridge inched toward the east. I couldn't see the brothers, but their shadows sparred against the cockpit sole. I shivered with an unnamable fear while, one by one, the nameless stars appeared. For the first time, I wondered about my life; I'd been careless of it before. But with care comes fear, such as when we take something fragile and newly fledged in our hands. I looked at mine, barely visible by the compass light, now that night was falling. With a finger, I traced the boat's name incised onto a brass plate on the instrument dash: *Psyched*. I didn't know what the word meant. But in Hannibal, I'd known psychics and mediums. I told you Marie Laveau could resurrect frogs and see the future in a crystal ball. (Miss Watson knew I'd come to a bad end, without benefit of any devil's instrument.) There was also Madame Ambrogio, to whom the spirits dictated prophecies concerning Armageddon and what your aunt in Topeka would be sending you at Christmas. During a tent show, Tom and I marveled at a Russian mystic in a pink-striped vest who could poach an egg with the heat of his gaze and scuttle spoons across the table by the power of suggestion. My favorite psychic was an ancient black man who could foretell the year of your death by the number of worm holes on an apple. After he was finished, he'd eat it for good measure. Jim used to throw chicken bones, but I was not convinced he had the knack of it. Christian teachings must have corrupted his finer animal instincts.

Was I gifted? I had "feelings" rare in a man, but not so uncommon in a child, especially one whose childhood spanned much of the nineteenth century and the entire twentieth. But I couldn't levitate, divine the future, dowse for water, invoke the devil (except my own familiars), or cause spirits to appear, regardless of how they would appear to me.

And rarely did I communicate by occult means with either the quick or the dead. Many years ago, I attended a séance. After a half hour's ungracious silence while we waited, in a gloom fragrant with lavender and dust, for a spirit to rap, I received a message—in dots and dashes—from Tom Sawyer. Having obtained a practical knowledge of Morse code in the Hannibal telegraph office, where smuggled whiskey and cigars were given to select boys in return for sweeping the floor and emptying the cuspidors, I interpreted the uncanny transmission in this way: *You will find buried treasure at* such and such latitude and longitude, both of which I intend to keep secret to safeguard a certain public official's prized flower beds from destruction. I did, in fact, unearth a mob of forget-me-nots and found nothing more valuable than a pair of old waders. Tom was ever a trickster.

Night had fallen like a scythe, as it will in subtropical latitudes. Our running lights shone on the black water, and James was following the channel markers into the harbor at Gulfport. We'd left Port Eads and crossed Chandeleur Sound to the Mississippi coast in six hours at a speed less variable than that of the raft, which might ply a river mile in minutes or in what seemed to Jim and me an age, according to aspects of time impossible to plot. I've tried to recollect how celestial bodies behaved during my childhood—the charmed one where my atoms were not obliged by gravity to move in ever-tightening orbits around the pivot, death. I can't recall what pictures the stars made against the sky, if the moon wore a lopsided grin during its phases, if meteors streamed from out of the farthest corners of space, or if the sun, in its day, arrived in green-and-rose bunting and, later, set in rags of red and gold. Tom would have sneered at such purple, but my imagination had fed on the Sir Walter

Scott novels he read to me. The night sky may be a perfect emptiness outside of time or, on the other hand, a crowding light; the day, a brilliance whose source is God or a supreme fission. (Or are the terrible secrets hidden in a dusk?)

That night, standing on the bridge with James, the stars told complicated stories in a language all their own. Had I kept dogwatch through the late hours, I might've seen the grinning moon sail across the darkness, showers of burning ice, and perhaps a golden planet advancing in a slow processional. James slowed the boat and brought her fenders lightly against the dock. Edgar and Edmund leaped from their respective places on the fore and aft decks and tied up to a pair of rusty bollards.

"How many knots did she make?" I asked James after he had turned the motors off. They grumbled a few seconds before giving up the ghost—a black and choking stench of diesel smoke.

"Eighteen, nineteen," he said.

"Can she do more?"

Boys love speed and recklessness. Long before this, I'd stretched out on top of a Hannibal & St. Joseph railroad car—the first in the territory—while the locomotive clicked down shining rails at eighteen miles per hour, raining on me sparks and cinders from the firebox. I tell you I was thrilled to death to move at such a speed! On the river, sometimes its banks would blur as the material world disappeared. I can't even guess how fast we traveled. Lishkovitz may have calculated time's escape velocity, but not in regard to a boy and a runaway slave on a raft.

"She'll cruise at twenty-three knots," James said. Had *Psyched* been a racehorse, he would have stroked her flank. "Wide open, she'll do twenty-seven or -eight, depending.

We fitted her with bladder tanks to carry extra fuel, which make her heavy. But she's got long sea legs! We won't need to refuel as often."

I wanted to know why we hadn't gone faster. I didn't believe in saving—money, energy, or myself for a future consummation. I spent what came my way as quickly as it arrived, squandered resources so as not to miss an opportunity. Mark Twain never understood the extent of my ambition. I was no ordinary Huckleberry!

"Best not to attract attention," James replied, laying a finger on his lips. "We've a long trip ahead of us."

Did I know what was hidden on board?

Not then, I didn't. And later on, when I knew, would it have made a difference to me? Would I have piped up in feeble protest or jumped ship and headed—where? Where had I to go? No, I would not have fussed. I confused natural probity with the lessons of the Sunday school. I did much out of spite for the self-righteous hypocrites who'd breathed their stale breaths down my neck. I wouldn't understand virtue until much later, when I was in love, which is also variable and absurd. Besides, I thought, what is the crime of smuggling compared to stealing a man from his rightful owner?

JAMES AND I WENT INTO TOWN to buy groceries. Edgar walked the marina docks in search of an adventure, which I surmised—by his clean shirt, freshly shaved face, and the bottled scent he'd drizzled on his palms and patted on his cheeks and neck—involved a woman. He was a good-looking rogue with an easy, indulgent smile of well-aligned white teeth. Edmund, however, was not one of those villains with a pleasing shape. He was unshaven and untended. His teeth were tobacco-stained, his fingers yellowed. His wardrobe consisted mostly of gray T-shirts and dirty dungarees. He was a misanthrope without a philosophy to justify his mistrust and envy of others. I hated him. Neither brother, I later realized, was much good; but Edmund was a dangerous good-for-nothing.

James?

Even now, I can't bring myself to judge him harshly, though he was a shady character whose choices had been motivated by self-interest. You could see it in the showy gold-clad tooth. But unlike Edmund, James was not vicious. I say this, knowing that he'd killed a man in Port-au-Spain and had to flee the island to escape the law and the vengeance of the dead man's relations. He had been a young man then—he was in his fifties when I knew him—but still, he'd given way to fury and searched another's innards with a knife. He may have had good reason. I never asked, and he did not know I knew. It was Edgar who told me because, I think, he was jealous of my admiration for the other man.

No, no, no! It was nothing like that! A man can be wounded by an unrequited love, whether for a woman, another man, a boy, or a dog. To think otherwise is not to have lived with open eyes and ears and mind. I liked James; I may even have loved him. Except for his name and race, he was nothing like my old Jim. But I couldn't help feeling that, in some way, in some measure, the one was dissolved in the other. Jim was sugar stirred into James, sweetening him. It makes not a particle of sense, I know. Answer this: Do you, my scribe and sounding board, believe anything I've said?

No?

Sometimes, one must tell an outlandish story because the truth is too fantastic to be believed. What I believe is this:

To read a book is not to experience life, but words—only them. But to say "only" is to underestimate them. Words in their sentences are a cosmography like arithmetic or the study of the stars and planets. I would not let you think that all these words—how many are there?

So many! I never guessed there'd be so many words, in rows and ranks, like soldiers in a forced march! Like automatons—cyborgs, they're called now—impressed into the service of a mind. But that is something I choose *not* to believe: I mean that all these many words I've bundled into the world are a logical result of consciousness and an autocratic will. I insist on caprice as a necessary countermeasure to slavery. Otherwise, my own dictatorial mind must take— unknown to me—its instructions from a mastermind. And I insist, as well, that this story tells a truth.

The Gulfport Convenience Store was an inglorious relation to the grocery in Hannibal where I had filched apples and walnuts. James seemed unaware of the poverty of its stock. Could it be that even Trinidad, which I had associated in my childish fancy with a natural largesse enriched by the swag of buccaneers, was, in 2005, also a fallen paradise? In many ways, the twenty-first century has been a disappointment to me. We go faster; we go nowhere. We live longer, only to be sick and disillusioned at our end. There's a chicken in every pot, with no thought to the suffering of the chicken. We consider ourselves lucky to have discovered, at last, ice-free routes for luxury cruises to an Arctic without snow or once indigenous life. We've applied the commercial notion of *wholesale* to death, which was sufficiently ample during the middle years of the nineteenth century. We have more geniuses than ever before, and the fruit of our genius is spoiled by the black spore of greed, murder, and catastrophe.

Would I have traveled back in time to pastoral America? (Notice, I do not say *innocent*.) No, life flows only in one direction, which is forward, and—moment by moment—becomes enamored of itself.

James filled the shopping cart with bread, cans of tomato soup, spaghetti, and tuna fish (with the nearby waters swimming with yellowfin, swordfish, grouper, tarpon, weakfish, drum, anchovies, sea trout, jacks, pompano, king mackerel, porgies, snook, red snapper, flounder, herring, grunts, and God knows what else or for how much longer), bottles of water and soda (cream, orange, root and birch beers), frozen hamburger, bacon, sausage, and boxes of doughnuts (jelly, cream, chocolate, and apple). He bought cigarettes in the brands favored by Edgar and by Edmund and, for himself, twisted cheroots soaked in bourbon.

"Anything you'd like, Mr. Albert?"

He always called me Mr. Albert. God rest his bones.

I put a corncob pipe and a foil pouch of cherry-flavored tobacco in the cart. Then I went to the rest room, though I did not need to rest, and splashed my own golden water onto a soggy mess of cigarette ends and wads of spent chewing gum.

James was waiting outside the store for me. Together, we walked home, admiring the soft night. I had discovered, while riding across the sound with him, that celestial observation was no longer necessary to navigation. The boat was equipped with GPS: Our positions and course were whispered to us by satellite. At the time, it was only another marvel to wonder at; but I've wondered lately what we may have lost by this device: a thread of light connecting our eyes to the sky. But I have—doubtless, you'll have noticed—a sentimental strain to my character. I used to fight it by pretending to be harder than I am. In years to come, I'd be a salesman and a sort of journalist; and both require aggressiveness to succeed.

"I bought you this," said James, taking from his jacket a paperback book. Pausing under a streetlight, I read its title: *The Adventures of Huckleberry Finn.* "You remind me of the boy in the story. Both of you floated down the Mississippi and smoked corncobs."

What else could I do except to thank him for his kindness? Did I read it?

No, but I pretended to, for his sake. It was kind of him. In fact, it was my first gift. Pap had never in his short, dissolute life given me anything but lickin's. Miss Watson and the Widow Douglas gave me useless things at Christmas, like scratchy mufflers, girlish mittens, and grammar school primers. James was the first to give me a present for no reason other than human kindness. *Human.* It's a word you don't often hear, except by way of extenuation for a minor transgression. *I stole my neighbor's ripe tomatoes from the vine, the hubcaps from his car, the wife from his bed—I'm only human!* Otherwise, you don't hear or see the word used much. Perhaps it reminds us that we are, like all other living things, a species.

Have I ever read Twain's book?

Recently, since coming here. I decided, at my age, it couldn't do me any harm. Twain took some liberties—I'll say that much.

James and I carried the groceries on board. Edmund was asleep on the sofa, a Mexican sombrero covering his face. A nearly empty bottle of tequila, lime wedges, and a hill of salt lay on the table. James took a pinch of salt and tossed it over his shoulder. How many times had I seen Jim do the same?

"Let him sleep it off," he said. "You can sleep in his state-room. I'll take the mate's cabin. Get a good night's rest. Tomorrow, we fish." He smiled at me and went below.

I guessed that Edgar had found company for the night. I felt like a smoke before bed and went outside and into the cockpit, climbed onto the bridge, packed my pipe with tobacco, and, drawing deeply on the stem, dragged sweet smoke into lungs not yet besmirched by tar or time. (Cankers of the flesh and spirit are unknown on rafts such as I had ridden.) The stars did not appear so hectic behind a haze of tobacco smoke, which calmed me and them both. We could be forgiven our weariness after so long an age spent in unceasing motion. I let the stars be, and looked toward Gulfport, whose lights were fewer now that night had deepened.

I hadn't known many people and couldn't help wondering at them—the human beings who lived on this edge of the continent, in a border town between elements. I wondered at the kind of life that went on inside its houses. Would I recognize it? I felt alien. And James, asleep in the narrow bunk, Edmund, inside some good or evil dream, and even Edgar, at rest in somebody's arms (it little mattered whose)—if they were to wake in the darkness, would they feel alien, too? We may as well come from Mars as from Earth, which we insult like rude and careless strangers.

You say I begin to preach too much? That my story is better told without anger.

Anger, friend, is the fuse. (So, too, is love.) And there is nothing like a pipe smoked in the small hours of the night to light it.

Far out on the water, a bell tolled. Its theme was a fitful, broken one: what a buoy performs in concert with an unruly sea. Straining, my eyes picked out a distant light, which came and went with the tilting surface of the Gulf. The wind had risen; I hadn't been aware of it till now. I shivered, and then I saw Jim.

Jim, my Jim! Surely, I've admitted to stranger things! All right, I *thought* I saw him—thirty or forty yards from shore—floating on his back, caught in a riptide. He was not lollygagging; he was traveling with a full head of steam, as if hurrying toward a rendezvous or a wedding. I remembered him as I had seen him last, at Waggaman, with no more life than a sack of pig entrails tossed onto a steaming ash heap. Only it was the river that steamed with humidity after rain. Jim became what his assassins always said he was: a thing. You must forgive an old man his tears. At my age, we cry easily. He would cry, you know—Jim would, turning his back on me, out of delicacy or shame. He had no more idea of manners than a post, but he was delicate in his feelings. You'd have thought he would have had every inch and particle of them beaten out of him.

Once, Judge Thatcher had to register a will in Jefferson City and took Tom along to see a dead pharaoh recently stolen from its tomb in Memphis (the ancient one). Egypt had been a craze ever since Napoléon's Armée d'Orient and the Battle of the Pyramids. The museum also had an exhibition devoted to Henry Darcy's hydrological experiments with water flowing through beds of sand. With his clever mind, Tom conflated water and mummies in what he called "The Hydrology of the Dead." Tom did have a highfalutin way with words! The gist of his theory was that the dead do not always stay put: They circulate according to principles of hydrology. The pharaoh in the museum had arrived at a point where past and present converged, as if washed up in

Missouri by time's ocean, in an expression of the conservation of momentum. To put it plainly, the dead are often wayward; and the drowned whose bodies are never recovered can be cussed and ungovernable. If Tom was correct, Jim, whose body was dumped into the Mississippi and never given proper burial, would circulate in the world's liquid element forever. It gave me chills to think of it.

I knocked my pipe against a rail and watched the ember fall and vanish on the water. Even the hardened heart must sometimes feel a prodding of the invisible and be moved, however briefly, by fear or awe. Whether because of Jim's revenant or a sudden oppressiveness of the magnolia-scented air, I understood that I had, in the quenching of that ember, witnessed a catastrophe: my death in its, the world's death in my own. My atoms may have started to decay, their orbits worn by age; but I was still only thirteen and could shake off anxiety as easily as I could a pesky fly. I went below and quickly fell asleep.

I DON'T LIKE FISHING. Oh, as a boy in Hannibal, I liked nothing better than to drop a length of twine into the river and lift out sunnies, perch, pickerel, and ugly old catfish, which looked at me out of goggled eyes, expressing an ancient weariness and disgust with the shenanigans of boys and the single-mindedness of men. I had no experience then of fish prized by anglers on big boats: sailfish, tuna, and blue marlin, which can weigh more than a half ton and had kept company with great whales when the waters of the earth were newly formed. (What of Melville's whale, which was hunted and harried into literature to become an imitation, a whale of words, or worse—a symbol?)

Edmund hooked a marlin the morning we went out to fish the Mississippi Canyon, forty miles off the coast. He spent seventy-five minutes strapped to the fighting chair, pitting his abject self against the fish's majesty, while James maneuvered from the bridge. Edgar praised and heckled his brother by turns, and I leaned against the gunwale, wanting to be sick. I dreaded the moment when I would have to yank the poor creature up by its gills. Not that I had strength to contribute much to a titanic struggle between the dominant species on land and that of the deep. Shoving me aside, Edgar would have to drag up the inert, broken beast. Fury and indignation spent, it gasped in the morning air, with a profound look of melancholy in its eyes I cannot forget. I don't know how long it took to pass into what constitutes the timeless dimension for fish. But when it did, I felt what the three Marys must have when Jesus finally died: a mixture of sorrow and relief.

Except for a horse blown apart at Vicksburg, I'd never seen death on this scale; and it shook me more than corpses of my own kind had done. To see this dead thing sprawled in the cockpit affected me as an elephant would, lying in the street, hacked to death with a meat hook. I'd angled up small fish with tiny hooks, which could bite a finger painfully; but the one impaling the great fish's mouth had the heft of a longshoreman's. Death has its measurement, and in our minds, we correlate torment with the corpse's size.

Edmund shambled into the galley to make his own sullen and solitary version of an occasion, with booze and potato chips dipped in a bowl of Chinese mustard. Edgar hosed the blood down the cockpit drain. I went up onto the bridge and sat next to James, who turned the boat toward Panama City, on the Florida Panhandle.

"You're white as a sheet, Mr. Albert," he said without derision.

I said nothing, unsure of his opinion of childish tears and flapdoodle. I had been as cruel as any other shiftless knockabout. I'd burned ants alive with a magnifying glass I stole from Judge Thatcher's desk; I'd scorched a couple of cats and visited death and destruction on a community of gophers. I'd slaughtered no end of innocent birds and varmints with my slingshot and never shed a tear. But here I was, sniveling and wiping onto the back of my hand the snot my nose seemed to manufacture, as if in mourning for all creation.

"When we get to Panama City, I know a little gal who'll cheer you up," said James.

"Who's she?"

"My own sweet little daughter."

James had daughters and sons scattered all along the Gulf Coast, spawned during youthful adventures as a smuggler of Trinidad rum and Brazilian absinthe, a deckhand and, later, a second mate aboard an oil tanker. He marked his children's positions on a map kept with his gear. Some he called dangerous reefs; others, happy isles. He was on friendly terms with three of his "wives" and liked to visit them when he could for a home-cooked meal and a familiar, warm, and fragrant bed.

"Her name's Sophie. She's about your age and wants to be a ballerina. I got a present for her."

We cruised more or less easterly toward the west coast of Florida, keeping well offshore—again, so as not to attract attention. Edmund butchered the marlin and stuffed the refrigerated fish boxes under the cockpit deck with meat. He kept a couple hunks to rot in the sun, which they soon did, and stunk. Is that the past tense of *stink*? I used to have a grammar book and a manual of style, but they're both long gone. I don't intend to say anything else about fishing, although we did fish a little each day for the sake of appearances. One dead fish is very much like another. If people want to read about the fishing we did aboard the *Psyched,* they can buy *The Old Man and the Sea.* This is not that kind of book. To be honest, I'm not sure what kind of book this is.

You want to know why Edmund left the meat to rot?

For the same reason Edgar bought me a dog when we got to Panama City. And for the same reason the brothers wanted me along on the trip to Atlantic City.

You think I'm giving too much away? That I should wait for a more dramatic moment in my tale than this, the tearful aftermath of a fish's destruction—all tension spent? Story line and fishing line, both gone slack.

Maybe you're right, and I should wait at least until we get to Panama City and the dog. Storytelling is all about well-timed revelations. But I'm annoyed by writers who manipulate me, parceling out information as though they were dealing dope. To hell with narrative strategy! The moment seems right to me—now that I've shown how inadequate a gaff boy and deckhand I was—to reveal the reason for my being on board. The brothers used me as window dressing, in case the Coast Guard boarded us. With me leaning on a gaff, like a shepherd in a Christmas play, we were likely to be taken for a party of sportsmen instead of marijuana smugglers. For days, the brothers had been conditioning me to call them "Uncle." (James was always James.)

The stinking meat and the dog? Edgar's idea. He reasoned they'd throw a drug-sniffing hound off the scent. He had a subtle intelligence for a former garage mechanic, waterman, and roustabout. Edmund's career was checkered with sojourns in reformatory and the county jail. What he did when he was at large involved—in their seasons—crab traps, a pick and shovel, supplying raw material to the proprietors of whiskey stills in the Louisiana backwoods. I don't know what this book is about, but it feels like it might have something to do with the embarrassing notion of goodness. And its apparent scarcity.

Do I believe in it?

I'm still undecided. A boy, I did not judge people as I do now, according to a complicated Hammurabi's code constructed of absolutes mitigated by fear, doubt, self-interest, and that "golden rule," the quid pro quo. A boy, I judged as the sponge or oyster does the water it imbibes: by recoil and painful shock or a vague sense of well-being. Children are unconscious of good and evil and remain that way until they reach the age of self-regard. The adolescent discovers a tiny universe of the self with his first pimple and plunges headlong into a lifetime of dubious ethical transaction with the wider world.

I thought of Edmund as a Morlock fattening on the Eloi, one of whom could have been his brother, Edgar. Edmund was gross in body and soul, gruff and stolid, while Edgar was fast on his feet, quick-witted, and eloquent in a rough-spoken way. I would not have called Edgar handsome, but he had a liveliness and a lightness of touch that made him attractive, despite the error of his ways. He was surely not the best of men, but he was hardly the worst. Edmund was a reprobate: a man to be wary of. When the brothers fought—they seemed to be constantly at each other's throats—I hid. James found their brawls amusing and would watch them scuffle like two bantam roosters in the cockpit. They fought over priority (Edgar was older by a year), percentages (Edgar wanted a larger one for having planned the job), and my value to the "consortium" (Edgar insisted I be paid a thousand dollars; Edmund wanted to give me nothing).

"He's useful," Edgar said with a coolness that belied the mounting temperature of his blood. He was slow to anger but would boil over without warning.

"He's a useless sack of excrement," Edmund grumbled, playing with his knife.

I was unnerved to find myself the fulcrum of their hate and went outside to James, who was putting a skirt on a naked ballyhoo. I watched his nimble hands thread the hook through the small creature's eyes and wished I were elsewhere—back in Hannibal with Tom Sawyer, playing tricks on Jim or the spiteful spinsters. Tom had been the brains of our operation, and it had been fine not to think much or weigh the consequences of our pranks. James's hands were scaly like the fish—from psoriasis. At that instant, he seemed part fish himself, whose element, like mine, is water. And by Tom's harebrained hydrological theory, Jim would swim throughout my life—and did, in James and in one other we have yet to meet.

"I'm sorry you got tangled up in this," James said, trimming the leader line.

I did feel an awful lot like a fish rising in a water column toward a baited ballyhoo and net. But there are motions that have an omnipotence impossible to resist—call them fate or accident or chance—fight them as you will. I was caught up! And maybe the bait to which I'd eagerly given my mouth had danced before my eyes way back when, in Hannibal, in water shining on the mudflats, or even before, in a spurt of Finn blood that came from my pap or his—conceived at the dawn of time, with the latching of a distant pair of chromosomes. Concocted in a primal ooze or, more remotely still, with the cooling of a star—its death and aftermath in me.

"Edmund scares me," I said.

"Of the two, Edmund's the less dangerous," James said.

That surprised me!

"He's a mean bastard you know you can't trust and have to watch. But Edgar's greedy and ruthless, too, only they don't show on him like they do on his brother."

"Edgar wants to give me a thousand dollars," I said, offering it as proof of his goodness.

"You don't have it in your pocket yet—do you, Mr. Albert? Besides, that's a drop in the ocean of what he hopes to make out of this job."

I wanted to ask James why he had signed on for it, but I didn't. I must have suspected even then that a smile and a pleasant word could be a pretty whitewashed fence around a house of horrors. I didn't want to know what James was like on the inside. I needed someone on that boat to admire. And—it's true!—I had begun to think that maybe Jim had gotten into James—was passing through on his way to who knows where—to look after me. I told you I was a romantic!

It may not have been Panama City where Edgar bought the dog. Last night, I was waiting to fall asleep and thinking over my story, when I remembered we had stopped for fuel between Gulfport and Panama City. It must have been Biloxi, and Edgar didn't buy the dog; he found it on the dock, licking grease from a hamburger wrapper. He was mangy, old, and starved—perfect for Edgar's purpose: to confuse the nose of dogs conscripted for the drug wars. Our dog, which I named Duke, fell overboard forty miles off Sanibel, near the Florida coast, and was eaten by sharks lured,

no doubt, by its smell. And so are man's devious ways confounded by nature or by chance. I had emptied my reservoir
of tears for the marlin; it had not yet been replenished by
optimism or hope. Duke went into the bloody maw, unwept
by me, although not unmourned.

Funny, how completely I'd forgotten Biloxi, its tumbled
houses and broken trees. It had vanished from the map and
record of my life. Memory must be a kind of radiation—
its source an unidentified substance in the human brain. It
weakens according to a rate of decay established by something chill and beyond all human warmth.

WE PUT INTO PANAMA CITY at the hour when the water
turns pale, opalescent—a bath of cobalt grains in suspen-
sion; the air and sky seem one and the same. To breathe is
to swallow the sea. At such an hour, we can believe in goodness, transcendence, and in the radiant idea of God. When,
on the raft, I'd asked Jim if he believed in God, he said he
feared Him. I thought he meant the terror I felt toward my
father. But no, that wasn't it. He feared He did not exist.
At the time, I wondered how so deep a thought could have
come from the brain of a slave. But who has more reason to
be appalled by God's absence than a slave?

Am I afraid?

I'm afraid to think about it—now that I am eighty-five
and failing.

James and I walked from the St. Andrew Bay marina
into Panama City. We left the brothers to wrangle over
money and Edmund's refusal to moderate his drinking.
Edgar worried that an instant of drunken uproar would
bring the police. His elaborate theater of normality could

be undone by a bottle hurled through the windscreen of a nearby boat or a volley of obscenity aimed at a woman on the dock. A pretty girl dressed in three lilac triangles had already caught his brother's eye while she walked her Pekinese past the cockpit. Edmund's sullen boozing seemed to increase with every mile. Two days earlier, he'd set fire to a saloon chair after falling asleep lipping a cigarette. Fortunately, we'd been out of sight of land, although the black smoke could have brought a Coast Guard cutter down on us. James was nervous—this man who was the embodiment of calm. Whether the cause was the impending reunion or Edmund's mutiny, I couldn't decide. Sophie and her mother lived in a low-income apartment house called Edgewater Garden, and we were expected there for dinner. But first, James insisted I get my hair cut.

"You look like hell, Mr. Albert," he said, ruffling my hair affectionately.

I never liked to be touched—especially in those days when the only person who had ever laid a hand on me was Pap, with force enough to smart. Anybody else but James would have felt my own hand's angry reflex. But I'd sensed in his touch only kindness and so let it pass. My hair really must have looked a mess: uncut, unkempt, unbrushed, and clean only because of the showers I took twice a day aboard the *Psyched*. I was learning to adore showers, sheets, and contrivances like a machine that washed the dirty clothes. The twenty-first century is a vast improvement over the nineteenth, I thought; and when James admitted he'd never heard of castor oil, I was converted to modernity.

He led me into a "colored" barbershop. There was no more Jim Crow—not even in Mississippi—but the color bar had yet to fall where men went for a haircut and a shave.

Segregated by reason of the intimacy of human hair and whiskers (abhorrent to some), a barbershop was a kind of private club where you could get whiskey, news, or even place a bet. I'd never been inside one and was intoxicated by the smell of shaving soap, wintergreen, sweet clipper oil, and eau de cologne, which a barber—a smart-looking gent with a thin mustache—rubbed into the crinkled hair of a man beside me. I sank luxuriously inside my blue-striped bib while my barber—bald and asthmatic—sought out James's eyes in the mirror for his tonsorial instructions. And then while he pumped a pedal near the floor, I levitated!

"Cut it all the hell off," said James, "and send the cooties to the museum of natural science."

The barber laughed and turned the clippers on. They growled once, then buzzed into life. He ran them deftly through my hair. I watched it fall, in heavy lanks of dirty blond. When he'd finished cutting and powdering my neck with talc, he swept "my glory" down a hole.

"Where's it go?" I asked, indicating with my itching nose the hole, like a trapdoor in the magic show I had seen with Tom Sawyer when we sneaked aboard the *White Cloud* the year before she sank at St. Louis.

"I sell it to the 'wig man,'" he said, and with a flourish, he twitched off my bib, whisked the cut hair from face and neck, stepped on the pedal, which brought me down to earth, and spun the chair toward the mirror—all in one fluent motion. In that motion, I saw—as I do always when watching practiced hands ply their trade—grace. Don't you find it so?

James paid the barber; I heard the register ring, the cash drawer shut with force enough to make bottles of hair tonic on the counter chime. I heard a barking dog outside and fell suddenly all the way back to Hannibal, to the shack where I'd lived with Pap. A barking dog—so slight and melancholy a thing—is a thread on which my memories, planets of my revolving days, are strung. To hear that bark recalls me sadly to the lengthening river of my years. It is a time machine that depends only on the human wish to visit what is gone.

James and I stepped out into the glaring afternoon and turned north onto Balboa Avenue. He didn't saunter the way he usually would to prove a nonchalance and superiority, but dragged along as if slowed by an invisible anchor. I guessed he was scared at the prospect of meeting Sophie.

"It's been nearly three years since I saw my girl," he said. "I wonder if she'll even remember me."

I said nothing, unqualified to speak to the loneliness and guilt of absent fathers. I was a boy, after all, regardless of my years and my bitterness toward my own pap.

"You know, Mr. Albert," he said, abruptly casting off his pensiveness, "you're still unfit to be seen in public. What you need next are some new threads."

I made no objection when he took my arm and steered us into a department store, its big plate-glass windows boarded over in the wake of Katrina. The threads I wore were those I'd found inside the crate, which had delivered me safely— remember—to the Venice *necropolis*.

No, I like the word! It gives distinction to a common graveyard. It makes me hopeful of a flourishing civilization after death, even if a somber one. I picture silent throngs minding their own business in a city of the dead, with streets and marble buildings, graveled paths and benches where shades sit and feed pigeons with crumbs. Real pigeons, real crumbs! I like it better than a picture of tombstones, like headboards for beds of clay and grass, in rows, reminding me of the children's ward where I recovered from a fever during my reform school years. We'll get to them in due course.

James chose a shirt—a gaudy thing bright with parrots—and a pair of loud Bermuda shorts. I tried on leather sandals and a yellow baseball hat. In the changing booth, I saw myself with a shock of *un*recognition, which staggered me. I'd seen my face before then: in mirrors on the boat and in the barbershop and long, long ago in shining puddles after rain. I remember coming upon my face, suddenly and for the first time, in a looking glass on Miss Watson's dressing table. But I must not have really *seen*, not with fresh eyes and a newly minted gaze. It may have been the clothes and the haircut. But I felt a dispossession and dared not leave the changing booth, for fear I'd leave my face and self in the mirror. Children become philosophers when standing in front of mirrors. They invent worlds and stories there.

"Albert! Are you done admiring yourself?" James called from the dressing room door.

I broke the thread of my stare, turned from the mirror, and went outside in my new clothes.

"You took your time," he said.

What a funny expression! As though time were mine or anyone else's to take.

James paid the cashier. I dumped my old clothes and shoes into a plastic bag. On the street, James looked his old self once more. Jaunty and swaggering, he walked briskly toward his Sophie.

Edgewater Gardens had neither water nor gardens, although there was a dusty palm tree whose roots had lifted and cracked the sidewalk during the hurricane; and there were bushes full of birds I heard but never saw. We went inside the brick building, climbed to the second floor; James knocked on a door, and in a moment Sophie opened it.

"Are you my dad?" she asked ingenuously.

"I am," he said, unsure of what to do with his feet except to shuffle them in the dust.

The girl's mother appeared in the doorway, wiping her hands on a towel, which smelled of shrimp.

"Come on in!"

If James had worried about his welcome, he needn't have. She—her name was Camille—smiled warmly at him. Her skin made me think of copper and syrup. A bruise-colored butterfly hovered where her ample breast began to swell above the halter top. When she smiled at me, I saw she had a "valentine tooth" like James's. Perhaps in Trinidad, troths were pledged with gold-clad teeth instead of rings. I looked at her hand; she wore a cultured pearl on her finger, but not a wedding band. I don't know whether she and James were married. I never asked.

We went into the kitchen and sat, without a prelude of drinks, peanuts, and small talk in the living room. Without asking, she ladled peppery jambalaya into our bowls. We ate and talked all at once. Afterward, she carried the dirty bowls into the kitchen, singing a Calypso song, while James poked foolishly at the girl, who laughed. Camille brought us more beer. The ice-cold bottles sweat and beaded; the bent bottle caps made a pleasant heap. Sophie got up on her toes and danced. I said little. What did I know of this life?

"I've got a present for you," James said, giving the girl the package he'd lugged all the way from the boat.

She tore the pink tissue paper from a walnut music box.

"Take it into the front room to play with," he said. "Mr. Albert, you go with her."

I followed Sophie into the living room while James led Camille into her bedroom.

The box unfolded into a stage for a tiny ballerina painted gold. Sophie wound a key, and the little figure danced one half of a Tchaikovsky pas de deux, her body reflected in a suite of mirrors. Sophie and I lay on the floor, her chin resting against her palm, my cheek against my arm. I couldn't take my eyes from the golden figurine turning in the row of mirrors, lit by an accidental slant of light that had traveled across a gulf of space as if with no other thought than to make my eyes grow heavy, my eyelids droop and close until I'd fallen into a trance.

Tom Sawyer had told me how, in a St. Louis music hall where an uncle had taken him and Sid for a birthday treat, a mentalist in a stovepipe and black frock coat tried to hypnotize him with a gold watch twisting on its chain in a sickly light cast by gas brackets. Tom was a difficult subject, he told me proudly on his return to Hannibal, able to resist the power of suggestion. Unlike my old friend, I have always been susceptible to another's will.

Sophie was telling me how pretty the apartment was—all lit up with candles during the storm—when I fell asleep on the floor. Was it sleep? It reminds me of what used to happen to our minds when, as boys, we'd breathe deeply into a paper bag: Our eyes would go dark and sting, and we'd swoon.

"Do you want to see my titties?"

Becky Thatcher was undoing the buttons of her blouse.

"You're Tom's girl! Get away from me!"

"Albert! Albert, you're dreaming!"

Somebody was shaking me. Tom. Tom, it wasn't my fault—it was Becky's doing.

"Wake up, Albert!"

I opened my eyes, to see Sophie kneeling next to me. Her blouse was buttoned. I've never been sure if it was she who'd wanted to show me her breasts, or Becky. Embarrassed by the knot of lust in my pants (Tom used to call it a "woody"), I ran outside. Night with its mockery of stars had begun to sift down over the town. I made up my pipe and smoked, wondering what it was, exactly, that James was doing to Camille and she to him. And all the men and women lying together under the roofs of Panama City (the wrecked roofs covered with tarps to keep out night and rain)—what was it that made them search one another out with their mouths and hands? Was it love or desire, human need or only fear?

"You all right, Mr. Albert?" James asked, sitting on the curb next to me.

The street was pitch-dark; the streetlights had not been restored since the storm, which had blown into me its turmoil and noise.

I nodded yes, mutely, in case my voice should shake.

"You know, Mr. Albert, this trip we're making—it's not good for you. They're using you, those Connery boys. You're part of a plan, Albert, to make us all look innocent. Do you know why we're going to Atlantic City and why we stopped here? We're delivering mail: marijuana, grass, doobie, weed, bud, cannabis, Mary Jane, kryptonite—call it what you like. The brothers thought a boy on board would make excellent camouflage. Edgar's smart. He figured the best time to run the stuff from Mexico to AC was right after a big hurricane. Coast Guard, cops would be busy looking after people who lost their homes. They'd have New Orleans and the levees to worry about. We crossed over from Tampico and slipped into a bayou near Port Eads just before the storm broke. We hitched the boat nice and snug to some big trees; the boys knew how to do it so she'd ride up on the surge without breaking up. Then we hunkered down inside an old cinder-block garage and waited it out. Afterward, it was like Edgar said: chaos and confusion. He'd everything figured, except his brother. I'm scared something bad's going to happen, Mr. Albert, and I don't want you getting hurt."

I listened quietly, taking comfort in the smell of cherry smoke and the pipe's taste of toasted corn cake. The stars hung over us like a spider's silver web. I could hear, behind me, Zydeco music playing from the window of Camille and Sophie's apartment. The moment was too rare for me to contemplate the brothers' treachery.

"I'd like you to stay here, Albert."

"Here?" I said, pausing in the contemplation of a cloud of tobacco smoke, which, instant by instant, was reconciling its contrarieties.

James nodded and went on. "I've asked Camille to take you in, and she's agreed. She's a good woman; she'll treat you like her own. You can grow up with Sophie—live like an ordinary boy."

Like an ordinary boy . . .

"Would you like that, Mr. Albert?"

I looked at James as Mary must have at the angel Gabriel. Can you imagine what his words meant, the altered life he'd organized and invoked? My resentment flared, but I dampened it at once. I realized this was not the moment for Roman candles of self-important rage. This man James had shown me what the world considers love. I cursed Pap for his folly in making me without it. Spellbound by his idea, James did not notice my mood's alternations of light and dark. I drew on my pipe, blew another cloud, took it out of my mouth, and smiled my earnest thanks at him. But I was not ready to be civilized.

"I'm sorry, James," I said.

He was a man of little education, but his apprehension was enormous. Like that other, older James, he had sensitivity, which Hannibal had considered an exclusive property of the well-bred and the well-to-do. Out of respect for my feelings, James never mentioned his glorious plan for me again.

WE ENTERED THE INLAND PASSAGE at St. Lucie Inlet on Florida's eastern coast. Norfolk lay 987 miles to the north. Most of the way was no wider than the Mississippi at Hannibal. I never liked the feeling of spaciousness one gets on the plains or on the open sea. Maybe because I lived my early years—those called "impressionable"—among trees that cloaked our lumber town and much of the river southward to the Gulf. Distant horizons and vistas without end dizzy me. Contemplating them, I feel unmoored. We cruised between marshy banks of salt grass and crowding cypress trees, under pale green canopies of oaks—slowing, while we passed weather-beaten hamlets and when the waterway turned from river to canal or widened into lakes incised by sailboat keels and water skis. We fished in the lazy fashion of backwaters, trading outriggers and the fighting chair for light tackle or hand lines. I put away the cruel gaff and marlin hooks.

Of all the days I spent aboard the *Psyched,* these on the Intracoastal Waterway were best. When the brothers quarreled, I left them the cockpit and climbed onto the bridge to sit with James. We were often quiet, which was fine with me. With James, I never felt obliged to speak. I talked, or not, according to my mood or the provocations along the way: a wading bird, thin and ungainly, shrugging off the weight of gravity to find its elegant form in flight; a huge carp broaching the water with a flash of gold scales; a deer, its summer coat glossy and chestnut, kneeling on delicate legs to drink; the burned-out ruin of a house or boat, showing gray ribs to the indifferent sun; and once, near Brunswick, on the Georgia coast, a drowned man draped with weeds as if in mourning for himself.

Edmund reached with a boat hook through the transom door and hooked the man while James idled the engines. The body lapped heavily against the stern with a dismal sound. Edmund turned it over; it wallowed in the trough behind us and then seemed to insist on its dignity by a show of calm disregard for our wake, Edmund's hook, and the unkind light, by which we saw how the water had bloated him, how time had turned him blue, and how crabs had gotten to his face and hands. I was sick in my yellow hat.

"Edmund, let him be," said Edgar.

Edmund obliged his brother by pushing the dead man away from the boat. The body was galvanized in a current, as if it had borrowed its will, and moved off.

"Shouldn't we take him ashore?" I asked James, who was tapping a fingernail against his golden tooth impassively.

"Can't do that, Albert. Can't get involved—not with what we're carrying. You know that."

I thought I detected spite for my having rebuffed Camille's generosity. But I knew he was right about the dead man, though I wished we could help him find his way to consecrated ground. (All ground is consecrated by rain and snow, by sun and the migrations of earthworms through the chocolate earth.) One man adrift in space and time is enough: Jim unburied is enough. James and I did not look each other in the eye. He pushed on the throttles, and the boat pulled away from that fatal intersection. I wanted to say some holy words but didn't know any, except for *Ashes to ashes, dust to dust,* which was what Tom Sawyer had said over the rigid bodies of frogs and cats. I spilled a little ash from my pipe onto the water. I had seen how death serves its summons on our kind. I was caught on the rack of time as I am now on the rack of my story, which is told in time and about it.

You say I should make it livelier, that it needs more action and less meditation. Fine, we'll rid the second draft of all annoying thought and embarrassing emotion. I'll tell a story—simple and plain—like "Big Two-Hearted River."

We went on and delivered mail at Savannah, Charleston, and Cape Fear. I angled for redfish, sea trout, bluefish, black drum, and Spanish mackerel. I lolled against the gunwale, half-asleep, half-afraid I would put myself under, entranced by shifting coins of light. Tired of fishing, I kept James company at the helm. Kitty Hawk was on our starboard side. Another pair of brothers, Wilbur and Orville, had flown an airplane on the beach below Kill Devil Hills in 1903 while Jim and I were on the raft. Their minds spun shining equations concerning lift, which unseated gravity; our minds— Jim's and mine—were luminous with history, which we had overleaped. The Connerys' minds were mired in base appetites. I looked at James and almost wished I'd stayed in Panama City. But there was no going back. We may not realize it, but every point during the passage of our lives is a point of no return—except for what memory permits.

"Do you think of Sophie and Camille?" I asked James, curiosity overcoming discretion.

"I try not to," he said without antagonism. "It's better to look ahead and imagine what's beyond the reaches than to cry over the past. Best not to get bogged down in it, Mr. Albert."

I have always fought the treachery of the past, which rises up and makes the present unlivable.

OUR LAST DELIVERY ON THE INLAND PASSAGE was Norfolk, Virginia. We tied up at an abandoned wharf north of the Campostella Road bridge. Edgar and Edmund put on mail carriers' uniforms and packed mailbags with cannabis. In Charleston, dressed as deliverymen, they had pushed orange-colored hand trucks stacked with bricks in shipping cartons. They were, at one and the same time, visible and not: the brothers, the boxes, the mailbags. This, too, was Edgar's idea, and you must admit its brilliance, regardless of your low opinion of him. I stayed behind with James, helping wash the cockpit, swab the decks, and polish the brightwork with chamois cloths. As I recall, we said little that afternoon, and I see no point in inventing conversation. Not now, when I'm hell bent on the truth.

The brothers returned in high spirits, their mailbags empty. Edgar set the day's *Virginian-Pilot* newspaper on the galley table. I saw the date and said, without thinking there could be consequences, "Today's my birthday."

James shook my hand and was pleased. "How old, Master Albert?"

"Fourteen."

"Happy birthday!" said Edgar, clapping me on the back. "May you live long enough to know better, as my old man used to say."

"Let's get the little shit laid!" said Edmund, who had, I saw, been drinking.

Edgar offered to finance my rite of passage. (Or is it *right*?)

I was reluctant; James, worried. "Fourteen's a little young," he said.

"Crap!" said Edmund.

"Fourteen's the perfect age," said Edgar. "He can see what his hand's been missing, and he's young enough not to have to shoot himself with regret. Isn't that right, Al?"

I nodded, afraid to do otherwise. How many boys have been sent to a woman's bed for the first time, unwilling and unfledged—carried there by a jeer or a maxim? James paced the saloon, not knowing whether to abduct me, break the brothers' heads, or give me one of his French letters. Edgar drizzled me with cologne, like a priest sprinkling holy water. Edmund guffawed and tipped back a bottle in a brown paper bag. The occasion was festive and might have been mistaken for a party, had I not been frowning.

"The kid still stinks," said Edmund.

Edgar must have agreed, because he pushed me into the master stateroom head to shower.

"I still say Albert's too young to be with a woman," James said while Edmund practically barked me with water jetting from the shower wand.

"He'll be fine!" Edgar snapped.

"You and Edmund better watch out for him," James admonished.

"Stop your clucking, Jimbo! We're Al's uncles, aren't we? You remember that, Albert, if anybody asks. You're with your uncle Edgar and your uncle Edmund. We've been driving the boat up north, after Katrina wrecked our house and landing . . . doing a little fishing and sightseeing while we're at it. You lost your folks in the hurricane."

"He's just a poor orphan!" Edmund said, relishing the thought of my bereavement.

"Your uncles kindly took you in, and we're going to New Jersey to visit kin. Now, let's get dressed."

Not even Tom Sawyer had experience with girls. Up until 1835, when I was ravished into timelessness, no one in our gang of ne'er-do-wells had slept with a woman, except an older boy named Ned Tolliver, who'd worked the previous summer on an Ohio River paddleboat as a steward. Well-favored and tall for his years, he caught the eye and fancy of a lady on her way to Cairo to attend a convention of spiritualists and mediums, convened by Andrew Jackson Davis, a seer and clairvoyant from Poughkeepsie. Ned and Miss Clara had what was then called "carnal knowledge" of each other; it happened in the lady's cabin when Ned came in to change the sheets. He claimed their entwined bodies had levitated a yard above her bed because of his spiritual magnetism. Tom doubted it was as much as a yard, knowing Ned to be inclined toward exaggeration and adornment. I expressed no opinion, being ignorant of spiritualism and sexual congress. I wondered what Tom would think of this escapade and wished he might speak to me in my mind the way he sometimes did. To tell the truth, I was afraid of girls and would rather have swallowed castor oil or a slew of fire ants than sleep with one.

We walked up Tidewater to Calvert Square—and damn if I didn't see myself on a signboard perched above a factory's roof! Home of Easy Chairs for Lazy Boys it said underneath a picture of Huckleberry Finn in ragged clothes and a straw hat, chewing on a sweetgrass stem, looking indolent and shiftless, with a TV remote in one hand, a glass of lemonade in the other. He was not an exact likeness, but close enough to make me feel again that loosening of self-definition I'd suffered in Panama City in the changing booth. I was distressed and in no mood to undergo the ordeal of first love. I would have slunk away, but the brothers, divining my intention, held my arms.

In the whorehouse, they pushed me up the stairs behind a fat and yellow-haired woman of middle age named Marigold. She cranked a replica of an old-fashioned gramophone and smiled when Conway Twitty moaned "I'd Love to Lay You Down" from its digital innards. I took off my Bermuda shorts, knowing by hearsay what was expected of a client. The quicker I get this over, I thought, the sooner I'll be back with James. She laid me across the bed and, cooing, saddled me with her hams. The sight of her gargantuan breasts (so very different from Becky's or Sophie's, which I'd pictured in my trance) scared the bejesus out of me. I looked toward my lap and saw my bird was shy. Chuck and chuff as she might, Marigold couldn't make it cocky.

"Sorry, honey child," she said. "Do you want to see my pussy?"

"No, thanks," I said, looking instead at a sickly goldfish in a bowl.

She shrugged, and her massy breasts juddered as if in prelude to a volcanic eruption caused by some titanic strain. She covered up and—maybe to give me my money's worth—took out a greasy pack of cards. One by one, she dealt out my future until, with a frown, she said, "It's the death-by-water card, honey."

True enough, if you allow for the ambiguity of the word *by*.

I went down to the parlor, passing a sailor on the stairs.

"They said not to wait," said a blue-haired woman with a cash box.

I left and walked the way I'd come, thinking, So this is

love. . . . The photo of Huck Finn—I will not call it me!—was illuminated by floodlights. He wore the stupid, self-centered face of a hedonist. I hated him and Twain and all else who expropriate another's life and mind. It doesn't matter we do not know our own. I wished I'd had a can of whitewash; I'd have climbed up and defaced the sign—blotted out that other boy whose destiny was crossed with mine.

So now there is another pair of brothers, I said to myself. Which is the bastard: Huck or me?

I kept on until I reached the boat. James was snoring gently on the sofa bed, where ordinarily I laid me down to sleep. I guessed he meant for me to take his berth. Maybe he knew I'd want to be alone with my sadness or my shame. I went below and, by impulse, looked in Edmund's stateroom. I don't know why, unless it was the thrill of fear to be inside an enemy's lair. I went through the wardrobe and dresser drawers. I didn't find a gun. I think I thought I might. I don't know what I would have done with it—thrown it overboard perhaps. I did find a stash of grass. I pinched some for my pipe. In the small aft cabin, I locked the door and, opening the portholes, smoked.

The night of my fourteenth birthday had been given over to novelty and induction ceremonies—so I told myself while I drew the acrid fume deep into my lungs. I took no more pleasure in it than I had my bout with Marigold. This story is not about innocence—its loss or maintenance—but about a child's becoming conscious in and of the world.

AT CHESAPEAKE CITY, on the Chesapeake and Delaware Canal, the *Psyched* twisted a shaft. We lay helpless, riding at anchor while the rain began to fall. James had dived with snorkel and mask to survey the damage, which was beyond his power to repair. Edgar looked at his brother anxiously. Edmund was an instance of the uncertainty principle: To gaze on him must be what an astronomer feels contemplating, through the telescope, the sudden gravitational collapse of a star from nova to degenerate dwarf. Or an immunologist at the birth of a new malignancy. You've known people beyond all reason and appeal—impenitent, irredeemable, insufferable. Edmund was one of those. As he swayed by the transom door, I wished Edgar—yielding to the fine rage I saw in him—would push his bastard brother overboard. There are no sharks in the C&D Canal, but the water is sufficient to the drowning of a drunken man. I'd have said *swine,* but the animal kingdom has never produced a lower specimen than Edmund Connery. If I'd found a gun on my birthday night, I would have used it now and given myself a belated present. Hatred is unattractive, but it's also irresistible. If men were honest with themselves, they'd admit it's a stronger passion than lust.

"Get below, Edmund!" Edgar growled. "And stop your damn drinking!"

Just then a Coast Guard utility boat came into view, and its captain hailed us.

"Just what we need!" said Edgar, cursing a tragic destiny that had spliced in an instant the threads of his possible downfall: a twisted shaft and brother, the Coast Guard, and the rain.

Quick as always on his feet, Edgar laid his brother out with the same wrench James had hoped to use to straighten out the shaft. He bled but little, to our relief. Edgar strapped him in the fighting chair and placed a pint of Tanqueray between his legs. Once again, I admired his flair for camouflage. An officer boarded through our transom door. He seemed annoyed.

"What's the trouble?"

"We twisted a shaft," Edgar replied, and nodded toward James, who smiled beguilingly and confirmed our situation with a helpless glance at the deck.

"I took a look, and there's nothing I can do," James said.

He emphasized his helplessness by kicking the diving mask across the cockpit sole.

"You can't sit out here all night. Where's your home port?"

"Just below New Orleans," Edgar replied suavely. "We beat out the hurricane, but our house was destroyed. We're running up to New Jersey to stay with family."

"That's tough," said the captain, softening. "Look, we'll tow you into Chesapeake City for repairs. What's wrong with him?"

While he had been addressing Edgar, he'd had his eye on slumping Edmund.

"Drunk," said Edgar; and to forestall the other man's next question, he went on hurriedly: "He fell and hit his head against the gunwale."

I could see the captain hesitate between a duty-bound pursuit of truth and his impatience to be gone and out of the rain. The latter won. He did look miserable, the water falling from his hat.

"There's a hospital in Wilmington. Will he live till then?"

"He's dead drunk is all," said Edgar, laughing.

"Get ready for the towline. You better get him below."

He returned to the boat and barked orders to his crew. James helped Edgar drag his brother below, then returned and climbed up on the bridge. Edgar followed him on deck and, receiving the tow rope from a crewman, made it fast. The captain boarded us again. Edgar blanched.

"Let me see your boat papers."

Edgar went into the saloon to fetch them. The officer scanned them and handed them back.

"They're in order," he said. And then he added, ironically, "People lose their boats in a hurricane to more than wind and water."

He went back aboard, and in short order, we were under tow toward a boatyard in Chesapeake City. That night, we slept on the *Psyched* while the rain increased and rattled on the hull and the canal water rose and lapped. By morning, the rain had stopped. The boat was trundled out of the water on a length of track that led inside a shed of grizzled boards, and her damaged shaft was pulled. The foreman promised she'd be ready in late afternoon.

The brothers walked along the canal: Edmund to find a barroom, Edgar to keep him halfway sober. James and I walked west on Boat Yard Road, then turned onto Lock Street, where, farther down, we came on a traveling carnival. You know the kind, with rides and stalls of redemption games and a line of tents with a tired barker announcing freaks. These were ordinary: scaled-up or -down versions of the human frame, stunted or elongated limbs, a man got up as a three-headed dog, and a topless woman lolling on a chaise longue, lazily flipping her mermaid's tail.

Once, Tom Sawyer had paid Hannibal's only certifiable lunatic to lie out on the mudflats, her top half naked, her legs and bottom stuffed into a canvas fish tail with painted scales resembling shingles. That was another one of his schemes to scare the daylights out of Jim. Only Jim became infatuated with her—an unforeseen circumstance that amused Tom endlessly. Poor Jim would moon about the mudflats by day and, carrying a lantern, at night, looking for his mermaid, who was never seen again. Crazy with rapture for this fabricated creature of the deep, he'd have stolen himself away from his lawful owner and forsaken his unlawful wife and children to be with a chimera, which, doubtless, would have broken his sad heart. I'd feared for his wits and stayed near him in case he should decide to drown himself for love. (Why a black slave and not I could have been made desperate by love is a mystery.) Standing in the tent, sweating with shameful remembrance and with the close and stinking tented air, I said to myself, I'm sorry, Jim, for the part I often played in your torment and for the pleasure I took.

I listened in my mind for an answer but heard nothing but the barking of the phony Cerberus standing guard at the gates of the underworld, scratching an itch on its behind. I was ignorant of all mythologies. I knew little about the life after this one, except what Miss Watson had rammed down my throat, chased with castor oil. But I sensed in the stirring of a canvas flap at the rear of the tent the presence of something uncanny and not of this world. There was a shadow there that swelled and shrank in the canvas folds. I recalled the white tent's flap at Vicksburg, which opened on a stack of Union dead. I was scared.

"Let's go," I said to James, who seemed to understand my uneasiness.

He had the gift, like Jim. Was it no more exotic, no more mysterious than sympathy? But what is more mysterious than this resonance, this etheric transmission whose source and purpose is affection?

Maybe the story I'm telling is just another one about love.

We returned to the boatyard in time to see the *Psyched*

float off the trolley into the water. The foreman started the engines and backed her into the canal in a cloud of diesel smoke. Satisfied with how she answered the helm, he brought her alongside the dock. James jumped aboard and took the wheel. I followed and, without a word, went below to think. Even a fourteen-year-old boy sometimes has to think. After a while, I heard the brothers come aboard and the boat get under way.

WE HEADED EAST ON A SLACK TIDE and left the C&D Canal below Delaware City. All was well as we hugged the Jersey side of Delaware Bay, dropping southerly to Egg Island Point, then southeast for the Jersey capes. Rounding them, we pushed into the Atlantic in a low sea and then northward to Little Egg Inlet, above Atlantic City: a seven-hour cruise from the C&D's eastern entrance. We left the ocean at Little Egg and crossed Great Bay to Bogans Cove—the end of our journey and of my childhood. The sun was nearly fallen over Goose Cove, to the west of us, while we tied up at a ruined pier behind an empty building where once small boats had been built. Its bricks needed pointing, the mortar mostly eaten away by rain and the salt air of the marshes; the roof was gone in places, and not a window had been spared the stones of rampaging boys. The place must have been favored by lovers. The cracked asphalt, annexed by blueweed, was sown with French letters—James called them "little socks of love"—where fugitive pleasure had occurred, rough-and-tumble, in the backseats of cars. A car parked beside the loading bay had its tinted windows up. Its cooling engine ticked as if counting down—a bomb about to detonate. James was uneasy, but the brothers walked toward the

car in a common delirium of greed. James and I remained
behind in the cockpit.

Yes, I need to do this right. It's my one concession to the
guile of storytelling. A climactic moment for the four of us
and a hinge on which the balance of my life will swing. An
accident—unless, as it did the sparrow, providence saw what
was about to fall down on us with the weight of inevitability.
None of us saw it coming, although James sensed something
in the air. It smelled of tidal mud and rot. He searched it with
his broad nose as if to scry our fortunes. Edgar and Edmund
were standing in a darkness cast by a corrugated iron roof
above the loading bay. Two men in suits were leaning against
the car; a third, the driver, stood opposite. Edgar turned and
whistled for us to join them. I started toward the transom
door, but James stayed me with his hand. I recalled seeing it
bleed when he nicked it cutting bait. Where was that? Near
Roanoke, whose first settlers vanished. I remembered my surprise at seeing the color of James's blood. Red. What had I
expected? I was such an ignorant and benighted child!

"James! Albert!" Edmund called. I thought it strange:
He rarely spoke to me, and only reluctantly or disdainfully
would he speak to James. "Some people want to meet you."

"You stay here, Mr. Albert!" James said in a low voice that
seemed to hiss at me. "I don't like the look of this. Keep your
eyes wide open. If you see trouble, you get the hell away
from here. Hide yourself in the marsh. Understand?"

I nodded, and with an enigmatic smile, he stepped onto
the dock and walked toward the car. I was seeing the last of
him. James was another who vanished from my life in time.
(But there are zones, remember, where clocks have no dominion.) I heard a car door slam, then angry voices, shouts, scuf-
fling. Edgar *goddamned* his brother, who had worked his knife

up below a rib. Edgar slumped against the car, then crumpled among the blueweed, shards of glass, and little socks of love. It all happened too fast to make a story of it.

James yelled to me. A shot was fired, another. I jumped over the side and slipped, nimble as a water rat, into the current. I let myself go into the dark and drifted noiselessly under stars aloof from the affairs of humankind. I crawled from the water up into the salt grass. In my hand, I clutched a brick of cannabis, wrapped in plastic. How I came to have it is a question I've yet to answer. The Connerys had set a brick aside to smoke on the trip home to Louisiana. With the money they made selling grass, Edgar planned to buy a fishing camp in the Delta; Edmund had something else in mind. Had I picked it up in my panic, or had James put it in my hand? So much hope and so much terror centered in a weed! Miss Watson had sworn by a cannabis extract manufactured by the Brothers Smith as a sovereign remedy for migraine. In the year of our Lord 2005, would she suffer her sick headaches or find someone in downtown Hannibal to sell her bud—a no-good shiftless boy perhaps?

The sun rose like an orange, having made its senseless round again. I knew in my bones that it did not rise for me. I walked along the shore of Great Bay toward the reddening horizon, for that was where the ocean was. On a grassy landing, I found a canoe whose aluminum form was made to look like bark. Whoever owned it was, no doubt, sleeping while the bleached blue air swirled and seeped into the house, invisible behind a stand of pines, whose scent reminded me of home. By "home," I mean the place where I was happiest: childhood, my first on the Mississippi, 1,263 miles above the Gulf of Mexico—a world, like the first settlement at Roanoke, now peopled by the dead. The world is new for each of us in turn; that's something we forget.

I took the canoe—a paddle had been left for me (by providence or by Jim, who may, in fact, be it)—and crossed a chain of little bays, over dead Indians' bones picked clean in whispers, south to Brigantine, where I got a job, of sorts, taking tickets in a fun house, whose theme was pirates—their ship and treasure. And so does each point in our lives refer to something previous. I think this is what's meant by déjà vu.

I sat inside a booth, unwinding pale blue tickets from a shrinking roll, and remembered how Tom Sawyer and I had heaved cardboard cutlasses at each other and how our childish hopes of finding treasure buried in the mud had been habitually dashed. (Once, we found the skeleton of a dog; the name on its collar was Duke.) Was it innocence or folly or an expression of the need to halt that made me show the roller coaster operator the brick of marijuana? Even now, so very many years later, I don't know what was in my mind, if anything at all. The next day, I was cuffed, shoved into the backseat of a squad car, arraigned, and, shortly thereafter, sent to the New Jersey juvenile detention center in Elizabeth. I would stay inside its walls until I turned seventeen and was sent back into the world to begin my life anew.

PART THREE

September 12, 2005–March 15, 2077

A FERRY ON THE HOOGHLY RIVER, tributary of the Ganges, sank on a night more than forty years ago: One hundred and twenty souls were lost overboard. (The soul, Naveen later assured me, cannot be lost—not for Hindus—but will merge, in time, with the Absolute. I thought of Jim, his body traveling the waters of the earth toward some Nirvana.) I was in West Bengal, staying with Naveen and his wife, Raima. He'd offered to introduce me to the president of an investment firm, the friend of a friend of his, who was rich and restless. At the time, I was a broker for Chronos Yachts, living in Palm Beach. Naveen and Raima had taken me to dinner on the river at Konnagar, near the ferry ghat. The night was pleasant as I recall, and we'd taken a table outside on the pier. A university lecturer in Bengali history, Raima was haranguing me on British imperialism and Calcutta. She insisted on its Indian name: Kolkata. Her resentment was evident. I was embarrassed and avoided her eyes, pretending to study a bowl of yogurt, until she mentioned a Rudyard Kipling story entitled "An Unqualified Pilot."

I thought of Mark Twain's book about piloting a steamboat, *Life on the Mississippi,* and of my own long-past river journey. Maybe Hindus are right to believe in a great circle of existence. I said elsewhere that each point in my life seems to refer to an earlier one. Maybe it's the same with the stories we tell.

A short while later—controversy silenced in favor of

fried moong daal—a commotion stopped us in midcourse. Diners rushed to the end of the pier (night's enchantment enhanced by twinkle lights) while a mob from the street descended on the ghat and, on the dark bank, pressed against the water's edge. I trembled, hearing the desperate blasts of the ferry's whistle before she rolled over—a stridency answered, in turn, by the sirens of nearby river traffic. I'm digressing, but digression is the soul of memory—which, at the moment, is my subject. I was fascinated by the big lights that swept the pitch-black river from shore and from the decks of rescue and firefighting boats, searching for the quick and the dead.

I see from your look, you think I'm heartless. You're wrong. That night while we stood watching the lights search the water, I was upset. *Upset* is too ordinary a word for how I felt in the presence of so much movement and emotion centered on stillness and silence: the place where the boat went down. But this tragedy happened long ago and what is left to me—an old man nearing his own still and silent point—is the image of searchlights crisscrossing the night-blackened water. It's a trope for memory. Like a brilliantly incandescent light, memory searches the darkness of the past for shapes and discovers them—haphazardly, if at all—one by one or in small, sad clusters: dim constellations of dead friends and loved ones, dead hopes and fruitless actions. Recollection is undone by vagaries of the heart, accident, the condition of our brains, livers, bowels. I worry that I haven't remembered everything of importance. We can't remember it all! There'd be no time left to live. But might not the searchlight roving my mind's darkness have assigned a false priority to some things, distorted others, made certain aspects of the past grotesque?

Time is running short. Let me finish this accounting with a few persistent memories, trusting in their authenticity and truth.

I HAVE NO WISH TO RELIVE the three pathetic years I spent under lock and key in the juvenile home, so called, at Elizabeth. First, there was nothing homelike about it; second, the inmates were too far lost to innocence, too sunk in grown-up vices to be considered juvenile. There is a third reason why this house of correction for scaled-down, small-time criminals is better left forgotten: Newark Bay. To be near it was an agony for a boy whose element and principal humor was water. When the air was heavy, I could smell it, although I had to root beneath complex odors of petroleum and— when the wind was in the southeast—landfill. Still, I sensed it and, like a caged animal, felt the energy coiled in muscles and tendons, seething to be discharged in motion. My heart was packed with an unassuageable desire to run, to swim, to take off my shoes and socks and wade. I promised myself I would never again be without open water, fresh or salt.

At first, they were inclined to doubt my story—the judge who sentenced me to the reformatory (to use a word fallen into disfavor, along with the notion of free will), the social worker, and the child psychologist. They didn't believe I was Albert Barthelemy, a boy raised up near Bayou Saint Malo by an old waterman who gave me his name after he found me floating, like Moses, in a cane and palmetto-leaf basket. I stayed with Albert until Katrina drowned him on his boat in the middle of Greens Bayou. I told my warders I had no other memories, except those of a childhood spent either on the water with my pap or else alone in a shack perched on rough-hewn stilts above the flooding marsh. (It would have been still madder to tell them the story I'm telling you!) They could find no trace of me in the Plaquemines Parish records. Either I was lying or the warrants of my existence had been lost in the hurricane. Confusion reigned yet in the Delta, and in the end, it was convenient for all concerned to accept my version of the story of my life. My identity as Albert Barthelemy was later confirmed by the sacred institutions of the Social Security Administration and the Internal Revenue Service. It was for me an irrevocable divorce, and Huck Finn retreated into the world of fiction.

Grieving, I read novels about the sea, borrowed from the "jailhouse" library: *Moby-Dick*, *Captains Courageous*, *The Sea Wolf*, *Lord Jim*, *Typhoon*, *Hornblower and the Atropos*, *The Narrative of Arthur Gordon Pym of Nantucket*, *The Cruel Sea*, and *Billy Budd*. (*The Adventures of Huckleberry Finn* was on the shelf—it has followed me throughout my life—but I didn't read it.) I was drowning—eaten by the salt of corrosive loneliness. I had no friends; no one to confide in; no Jim in his own skin or—by the mystery of transmigration—in another's. In the perverse way of a child, I would behave insolently to increase my isolation. I'd give my jailers no other choice than to punish me with solitary confinement. We will sometimes reach a point when the only antidote to pain is more pain. Have you noticed that? I have no wish to dwell on the sorrows of those years.

You're right. They were, by and large, self-inflicted sorrows. My sullenness and refusal to acknowledge the threat of the delinquent boys testing me for weakness saved me from the common curse of hazing. I was feared by some and thought crazy by others. For the most part, I was deemed unworthy of tormenting or befriending. I went my own way. And so one year yielded to the next and that one to the third and last of my captivity. I thought of myself as a frontier boy carried off by hostiles and made to practice savage customs, wear paint, and sleep in army blankets infected with typhus, as sweet a gift as the poisoned dress Medea gave to Glauce. (My mind imagines torments devilish as Torquemada's.)

Enough of this. I've wasted breath already on that court-ordered sandbagging—breached, in time, by time's irresistible flood. And *breath* reminds me of a fourth reason I hated those three years: They took away my corncob pipe!

The day of my release arrived. All things—good or bad—do finally come, whether we wait for them or not. They are the stations on our way to Calvary, or paradise. But before I leave the year 2008 forever, I promised to tell you about my six days in the children's ward.

See this tattoo on my arm? Looks like a bruise. Time has made it nearly illegible. It's a man-of-war that sailors in my day had needled on their arms. I was reading *White-Jacket; or The World in a Man-of-War*—another Melville novel in the library of the "juvie" home. We had plenty of books—most, undusted and unread—donated by the widow of a judge who had presided over the Union County family court. I can still see his name on the bookplate: *The Honorable Edward Renn.* I pictured a thin, dried-up man like a specimen in a taxidermist's shop. Years later, I sent a thank-you note to his widow, who kindly sent me back a photo of her late husband. He looked nothing like the household wren that had nested in my mind. Isn't it always so? We're confounded by the chasm yawning between what is the case and what we believe it to be.

The tattoo?

I did it myself with a tattoo gun I made with a tooth-brush, guitar string, empty ink pen, and an electric motor scavenged from a tape recorder. Most of the "JDs" did the same, but mine was the only man-of-war. I waited for the scab to heal, to show it off; but my arm got infected, badly. Sick and feverish, I was taken to a hospital with a ward for convict children. I was put to bed next to an older boy who'd lost both legs under a freight car during a rumble. He'd been a gang leader famous in Bedford-Stuyvesant for his knife. I recognized Huck Finn in him as he might become—stumps weeping into plastic bags.

Delirious, I remember dreaming about a pig dressed in a white nightshirt and cap, living in a little white house. It was night, the sky pitch-black, with a moon that would drift over the pig's roof. There was a noise, like a wasp. The pig would come out his door and, picking up the house, carry it from under the moon. But when the pig went inside again, the moon moved over his roof. On and on it went till I woke—pajamas drenched in sweat. I felt better, and next day was sent back to finish my sentence. I sometimes think my fever's cause had to do with my withdrawal from open water; I'd burned up in its absence. Sentence at an end, I left that hatchery of neuroses and the wish for death and went to work in a boatyard on the Jersey coast near Tuckerton.

Ms. BOWERS, THE SOCIAL WORKER who had overseen my rehabilitation (as complete a one as the intractability of my genetic inheritance allowed), had found a job for me that she judged compatible with my rearing and my reigning interests. I rented a room in Tuckerton, above a secondhand store, and began, like Horatio Alger, to rise. I swept the factory floor, learned to lay up fiberglass, became, in time, a member of the engine crew. I discovered I could talk to anyone and, like the late Edgar, was quick on my feet and—dare I say it?—charming and urbane. By the time I turned twenty-eight, I was selling the boats I'd helped to build—ironically, to New Jersey fishermen who traveled the Atlantic Intracoastal Waterway to winter in the Florida Keys.

Frankly, the memory of my sales career bores me. I regret those fifteen years as lost. I was not myself. I wore Italian shoes and shirts, drove a Maserati, smoked Turkish cigarettes, bullied and blandished on my mobile phone, sent vapid messages by Twitter and text. My God, in my thirties, I wore my hair in dreadlocks! It was a waste of spirit when I never once saw Jim or heard Tom's voice. I was being punished, I suppose, for having renounced Huck. I had let him go willingly, and my deepest self was in revolt against the person who had, for reasons of self-government, usurped it: me. I'd walked away from the mirror, leaving Huckleberry to languish in an imaginary room. I was conscious of none of this, of course. I sensed only a dissatisfaction with my life and a disapproval of all who resembled me. In a word, I was unhappy. Meanwhile, the true center of my life as a man lay 3,500 miles from New Jersey, in the Netherlands. I tell you, I long to break off my story here and now and take up the thread again in Holland, in 2034, when I was forty-three. But you would carp were I to leap, summarily, across the Atlantic without an acknowledgment of the intervening years. I'll be brief, as befits a waste of time.

I excelled in turning a vague interest into desire. I succeeded because I understood desire. I did not sell boats so much as seduce men and women into wanting what lay behind the words I spun from endless spools into stories of glamour, adventure, sex. I created illusions of a reality as palpable as a rabbit lifted by its ears from a magician's hat. In the common parlance, I had the touch; money first found, then sought me out, the way money does for some few people who know how to price and sell a dream. I taught men and women to want what they did not need.

In my late thirties, I sold my deep understanding of human vanity and self-love to a builder of opulent superyachts. I'd handled million-dollar fishing boats; now I would broker vessels ten or twenty times more costly. I moved to Palm Beach and enriched myself. I wore suits handmade in London by Burberry Prorsum and traded my corncob and Virginia burley for a meerschaum and Dunhill's deluxe navy rolls, which I lit with a Ligne pink-gold lighter instead of a locofoco. I lived with a woman who saw herself as a canvas for the artists of haute couture; her husband was serving time for a Ponzi scheme. I lavished her with expensive gifts and amorous glances because they were her raison d'etre, while I sold 120-foot boats to a prime minister, several princes of the realm, assorted oil magnates, financiers, industrialists, entrepreneurs of social media—and, once, to a sheik who kept his yacht in the waterless Sahara, cradled on a pair of railroad trestles painted gold.

What had made me so consummate a salesman?

My perfidious childhood—in time and out of it. My apprenticeship with masters of flimflam: Tom Sawyer, Edgar Connery, and many another well-dressed and well-spoken rascal.

In the summer of 2034, I crossed the Atlantic in a 150-foot yacht: the first of its size built by the company. We were delivering it to the king of Spain, who would exchange our captain and crew for his at Gran Canaria.

His obsession was big boats, especially fast ones like the Chronos 150, which had sea-trialed at forty knots. I planned to remain on board while the king cruised from Maspalomas, north across the Bay of Biscay, then through the Channel to Rotterdam. There, I would leave him to his affairs and see to mine in Papendrecht, near Amsterdam, at the office of our naval architect. Each year, I met with him to convey the wishes of our owners concerning alterations and enhancements to the line. He—his name was Willem van Oosterzee—adored De Stijl, whose vibrant austerity was felt in his designs for boats, as well as in his swank building overlooking the river Merwede, with its Gerrit Rietveld chairs and two Theo van Doesburg oils. Willem was himself sleekly dynamic and taught me much about modern art and music and—a Dutch fixation—herring and gin. I enhance the former with mustard, the latter with four drops of Angostura bitters.

You see how precious I became in middle age. Twain, if he could have recognized Huck in me, would have hated my guts. But the "Territory" Huck had lit out for in 1835 developed, in two centuries, into a country beyond the recognition of Americans who endured much for their own sake and for that of your contemporaries pledged to the self and its constant aggrandizement. We became a nation of pleasure seekers; not all, of course, but enough to form a constituency with strength to pervert the virtues of democracy. Debasement may have been inevitable; perhaps there was a fault line in our nascent character that money and the pursuit of happiness opened wide enough to engulf and darken all our hopes.

You don't believe it? Read de Tocqueville or Mr. Lincoln's second inaugural address and then read your morning newspaper. But readers of this ebb and flow of memory want to hear about the Canary Islands and the king of Spain. About wealth, power, and indolence, for which men and women should—with laudable obsession—dedicate their lives and the sacred blood of others. In the year 2077, ambition is our principal virtue. I wonder if it was always so.

THE KING OF SPAIN WAS NOT MY FIRST BRUSH with royalty: I had wrangled props and scenery, deloused Juliet's horsehair wig, and represented a retinue of retainers in several of the duke's renditions of Shakespearean drama during my youth—the one Mark Twain chronicled. Of course, the duke's pedigree was not so pure as that of King Juan Carlos, the—I have forgotten his regal denomination. We hit it off, the king and I; and after an hour's fawning, I was allowed to call him Juan.

He treated me with respect, serving up additional proofs of a democratic spirit by dismissing the crew and making me a Spanish omelette in the galley of his new yacht—he named her *Canción de Luna*—and pouring me, with his own immaculately manicured hands, a pleasantly chilled Jurançon. We sat on the sundeck, smoking fat Havana cigars, having bitten off their ends in easy fellowship. I told him a story of my life, and then he told me his.

He recalled with tender yearning a young girl met by chance in a tapas bar in Barcelona's El Raval Bario. Like the prince in another of Twain's books, Juan Carlos had given his bodyguards the slip; and disguised as a stevedore—or else a movie usher, I can't quite remember which—he ate chopitos, prawns, and fried quail eggs on bread, washed down with beer, with his pumiced elbows on the sticky tabletop.

While returning from the *cuarto de baño,* he collided with a waitress carrying plates of empanadillas. They became lovers soon after Juan Carlos had stooped to pick up the sardines in onion sauce, the broken pastry shells and plates.

"I was with her only the one night," he said wistfully. "In the morning, I was once again *el rey.* I never saw her after that, but perhaps she realized her good fortune when, later on, she received the key and title to an Aston Martin. It was used—by my father—but very gently."

Moved by an insurgency of desire, he went inside to be alone. I sat on while my cigar burned toward extinction and—as if to spite all handmade sources of light and comfort—the stars emerged, repeating for me their familiar patterns on the sky. I, too, yielded to the past: a night in 2005 when I had sprinkled ash in memory of a man drowned on the other side of the ocean. Unsettled, I dropped my spent cigar into an Atlantic warmed by Africa and the Sahara, heard it briefly hiss, went inside, and— undone by weariness, wine, and the ocean's drubbing on the hull—was soon asleep. I fell down into the unlit ocean, where vague shapes combine in dreams, and wondered why, unlike the king, I could not summon even a fleeting memory of tenderness with a woman. Not even for—no, I won't say her name. She's alive yet, in Palm Beach, and litigious when it comes to former lovers, which are many.

There was—about our trip north along the coastlines of Morocco, western Portugal, and Spain—something nearly magical. The *Canción* behaved as though she had passed directly from the brain of the naval engineer who drew her hull to the ocean, without need of any other construction than that which happens in the mind. She was the radiant *idea* of a yacht. Her engines were a dream of thrust and ascendancy, lifting her bow into the topaz sky while her stern drew an ever-widening vee behind us.

"She moves like a logical argument from one shining term to the next, toward an ineluctable end," said Juan Carlos, who was, during the space of that journey, changed, like someone in a spell.

He spent the time, which seemed unmeasurable, on deck, playing shuffleboard or shooting skeets, or inside the cabin, feeding Spanish coins into a slot machine or playing the piano. Astonished, I listened as he moved effortlessly from "Chopsticks" to Debussy's "Poissons d'or"—this man who had been tone-deaf since birth. Finished, he stood for my ovation, which I gladly gave, while a señorita dressed pertly in a sailor's blouse showered him with roses.

Wanting to be alone, I went outside and, sitting in a deck chair, watched the western ocean turning gold. It was then— I swear!—I saw Jim cradled by a golden wave, wreathed in a Stephen Foster song. His course, unaltered by the prevailing current, tended toward the place of his birth: Africa. He may have hoped to find his wife and children there. On the raft, in the shade of the lean-to, during intimate and earnest conversations with Henry Wilson, Jim might have heard of Marcus Garvey's Back to Africa movement. I didn't blame Jim for turning away from his countrymen; after all, he'd been enslaved and lynched by them. Seeing him now recalled me sharply to our common past: a shapelier time, a happier one for me, though not for him.

Thank you for this dream! I shouted in my mind, so as not to disturb Juan Carlos, who had gone below to the royal suite in order to savor his.

How marvelous it is sometimes to feel the minor agony of a broken heart! (I supposed this to be true, for I had yet to undergo love's trials, however much I knew of its lunacy.)

Jim vanished into the east, where sky and water had turned dark after the departed sun. The moment when day's effulgence suffers its eclipse is terrible! I was harrowed by a thought, perhaps because of it: What would become of Jim, or any other creature cursed with immortality, if the world were destroyed? Where all is naught, what space can an immortal occupy—what ground is left to stand on? A chilling thought made all the more so by another: Suppose Huck Finn is immortal, too, as experts in literary history have declared him? Does it matter I've left the role and changed my name to Albert Barthelemy?

You want to know where this is leading.

I may not have escaped Huckleberry Finn. You've heard of people unusually amenable to suggestion, who are regressed by hypnosis to other, earlier lives, as if the self were an archaeological record of personalities that disappeared without a trace until—by patience and exertion—they are, one by one, unearthed. Huck may be waiting underneath Albert Barthelemy for the final call to bring him, smartly, forward. Huck's personality may be the stronger and, in the end, may have power to overthrow my own. Perhaps Huck can better endure eternity, or the grave. Should I send for a hypnotist to release him, the way devout Catholics do a priest to daub their brows with the olive oil of Extreme Unction? Ought I go into eternity as Albert Barthelemy— or will I stand a better chance as Huck, who was less fastidious and scrupulous than I have become at the close of my days? And what if there is a still deeper antecedent self beneath us both, whose name might be Mark Twain? Had I tried to outrun the past, and failed?

I woke, feeling anxious and afraid. The king seemed not to know me. At breakfast, he was curt and, when I called him Juan, rebuked me for an insolent disregard of etiquette. After his toast had been reduced to crumbs and his coffee to its lees, he stood—on his dignity—and left without another word, allowing me to consider what was due a king. The steward reassured me, saying that his majesty often became sullen when he remembered the race of Spanish bulls, now sadly extinct. At Rotterdam, the *Canción* docked with an undignified bump against the pier. I rented a bicycle and pedaled the twenty-one kilometers to Papendrecht.

I MET JAMESON—BY ACCIDENT—at the Golden House in Papendrecht, where Willem and I had gone to eat dim sum. She was by herself at a table placed beneath a painting of the Yangtze River, elegantly conducting with chopsticks an orchestra of dumplings on her plate. Willem asked if we could join her. She smiled agreeably, and when two additional places had been set, we sat. Bashful for a reason I could not explain, I fiddled with a spoon while Willem introduced us to each other:

"Jameson Tarn . . . Albert Barthelemy."

"How do you do," she said, her eyes sounding mine, which slid away to a calendar by the kitchen door. I read the date, as if to steady myself in time: August 15, 2034.

Willem nudged my ankle with his shoe. I turned my face to hers and stammered, "Glad to meet you." And I was! As absurd as it must seem, I was pleased to meet this lovely black woman with a frankly penetrating gaze that searched for something in my eyes throughout the meal.

All right! It's far-fetched, but I believed from the first

instant I saw her that she was Jim. No, that's too disturbing an idea! Let's say instead that I believed Jim had entered her. That's not exactly right, either. I believed Jim had been *infused* in her, the way tea leaves are in boiling water, to become what is neither one nor the other, but something tonic and strengthening. In other words, Jameson—by an unimaginable transubstantiation—had acquired a vital aspect of Jim, who meant to look after me in death as he had in life. He may have fallen in with the *egun,* spirits of the dead for the Yorùbáns, who believe the border between the spiritual and physical life is porous. Fortunately for my readers (to speak optimistically), in 2077 I can talk of numinous states without fear of ridicule. In previous ages dominated by a vulgar materialism, I could not have told this story. (I'd have had to tell some other to explain my life.) But I want my readers to understand that when I fell in love with Jameson and she with me, there was nothing unnatural in our feelings.

"You have an unusual first name," I said later, when we were walking along the Merwede.

"My father named me after his favorite whiskey," Jameson said, and laughed.

"Willem said you were stranded."

"I am, although Holland is a lovely country to be stranded in. I chartered a cruiser at Rotterdam and planned to travel the Merwede to the river Waal, then on to the Rhine. But at Papendrecht, the captain took sick. His appendix burst, poor man. He's in the hospital. I'm thinking seriously of giving up and going home."

"I have my captain's license," I said, and, noticing her doubtful glance, added, "I've spent more years on the river than you'd think to look at me."

There are no coincidences, Tom Sawyer whispered in my mind to bedevil me.

"You have time?" she asked.

"As much as you need."

Time, for me then, seemed all but inexhaustible.

We walked in silence along the river—she looking thoughtfully at the water, I shyly at her face in profile, which stirred in me memories of other elegant lines, like a heron's in flight or the prow of a riverboat in the charged instant before getting under way. I suppose I was thinking of a quality as elusive as beauty; I mean *expectancy*. Isn't it marvelous how, with the speed of light, we can be recalled from the present to a commensurate moment in the past? And just so did Jameson and I arrive at a band shell on the riverbank—empty and silent now, but able to unearth an evening buried long ago when Tom Sawyer, Jim, and I stood by another river and heard a brass band playing military marches that had incited men to fall at Austerlitz and, on our own shores, at Dearborn and Detroit, on ground made noble, or ignoble, by death.

"People have been kind," said Jameson, her eyes resting on mine, which this time didn't flinch from hers. "Even here: Willem and now you. It's enough to make me believe in providence."

"Or accident," I said, feeling obliged, again, to resist the tyrannical persuasion of fate. (As if it matters to the body mangled in a car wreck whether the fault lies with fate, accident, or a moment's inattention!)

Earlier, I mentioned that something had changed me: an accident I had no earthly reason to expect. Do you have the passage? Yes? Let me see it. *I was changed, too, by something that I will insist, always, was accidental: an instant of*

*senselessness and absurdity when I fulfilled the river's purpose
and my own.* I was talking about Jameson and the impetuous
moment on the Merwede when I offered myself as captain
and she just as impulsively accepted.

IN SANTA MONICA, WHERE JAMESON wrote and illustrated
children's stories, she'd had the happy thought of turning
a pilgrimage to the German town of Münchhausen into a
picture book. An eighteenth-century baron by that name is
famous for his fantastic tales and became himself the subject of improbable narratives like *Marvelous Travels on Water
and Land: Campaigns and Comical Adventures of the Baron of
Münchhausen.* She'd planned to follow the Merwede's more
or less easterly progress to the Waal, then on to the southerly tending Rhine. Below Koblenz, she'd travel the Lahn, a
tributary of the Rhine, northeasterly to the Wetschaft valley
and the town of Münchhausen. It was not until she hired
a boat and captain in Rotterdam that she understood her
intended journey's impracticability. (With its feints and
twists, the river system seemed a folly to me, who was used
to the frank ways of the Mississippi.) The captain soon persuaded Jameson to forgo a trip to Münchhausen in favor of
the Middle Rhine and its castles.

"It was a disappointment!" she said to me. "Still, there's
no reason why I can't honor the baron with a marvelous
travel story of my own."

She'd turned the smaller stateroom into a studio, where
I discovered pencil sketches she had done between Rotterdam and Papendrecht. She had a gift for capturing, in barest
summary, small moments that promised larger things. Her
line was confident; her shading conveyed an absence made

mysterious by an almost-glimpsed presence. She'd brought a number of her published books. One in particular, about a boy and a giraffe named Rupert, moved me by its unchildish refusal of sentimentality. It began: *From autumn until spring, I left the attic just once—to go to Africa with Rupert, my friend. There was a war. Smoke darkened the sky. At night, it covered the moon. We were afraid. The attic belonged to a man who made shoes.*

I don't propose to recite the itinerary of our river journey, my last, as it turned out (unless another awaits me beyond time's final reach). In any case, I don't remember the places where we stopped. My thoughts were centered on Jameson, who was herself the beauties of the way. I can't recall the rails on which we slid, according to love's commissioning, from affection into attraction. Like the rivers themselves, the passages down which we moved were unmarked. We struggled at once to cleave and to fend off—the countervailing motions of the bewildered heart.

I do remember the drawings she made while the boat took us deeper into Europe and ourselves: a boy tying a rope to a deck cleat, a boy at the wheel, a boy—always the same boy, whose given name she made my own: Albert. Albert opening a canal lock; fishing with a net for eels; reading in his berth; shivering after an evening's swim in the Rhine. There were many other drawings—all framing the boy as he traveled, like us, on rivers that became increasingly uncertain of their course. Life—even one as long as mine—had left me unprepared for love. I realized with a start that I had never before loved anyone, except maybe Jim. I kept an eye on the river, whose bends followed hard on one another much too fast to be careless at the helm. But I was helpless not to steal a glance at

Jameson as she sketched and smudged, scrumbled and grumbled over her failure to seize with her pencil what her eyes saw. She took a miniaturist's delight in details: of the boat, a weathered pier, or an elm branch, still oddly leafed, lumbering along in the current. She was transfixed by the story unfolding—in pictures and in words—while the river unfolded from reach to reach. At night, we tied up to the bank or, when the river was wide enough, moored out toward the middle—the better to be alone.

You will have read enough about love to make the recounting of mine unnecessary. Passion bores me; maybe I'd think otherwise if I were not an old man. I'm not sure I can speak the language now. I wonder if I ever could with the effortlessness of those who do not seek each other in the dim bowers of their selves, but, rather, in sunlit uplands— or on a boat traveling between untroubled shores. We must have stopped often during the three hundred miles of that fateful, if uneventful, trip. (God-damn the unalterable courses it seems our lot to bear!) We halted for fuel, food, water, to stretch our legs. But I can't recall anything other than a sensation of contentment and a genial peace. Jameson and I might have been in the peaceable kingdom painted by Hicks, speaking to each other in the sensual language promised by Jakob Böhme, for all I remember of the way. Doubtless, it had its excitements. After all, I was in love, although I've never known the fits and seizures of a heart besotted like Jim's for his mad mermaid of the mud. Mine was joy in a quiet harbor. All the same, the journey was marvelous. Not even the hyperbolic baron could have imagined one more marvelous than ours. I was entranced as I had not been since the days on the raft. But time tick-tocked on the Rhine as it had not on the Mississippi for Jim and me.

You want to know about our rough-and-tumble in bed, on the ottoman, the deck chair, and foredeck sun pad? Forgive me, but I haven't juice enough to indulge a salacious interest. We had sex, naturally. Leave it at that.

"Have you read *The Adventures of Huckleberry Finn*?" Jameson asked me one night while we lay in a drowse, listening to the stiff noise of reeds scraping against the hull, the soft music of water lapping there. The portholes were opened to the night, which stole into the cabin, already nervous in the wavering tides of shadow. There was something in the air: a disturbing odor compounded of sluggish water and compost.

"No," I said, and quickly changed the subject in order to be rid of the hated book. "Tell me the story you're writing. What's it called?"

"*The Boy in His Winter*," she said. "At least, that's the working title."

I thought that strange and asked her what it meant.

"The story's told by an old man looking far back into the past at his boyhood. From that vantage, he can see things clearly without the haze of childhood to soften and alter them."

She was too young to know how old age also has a haze that can dissemble, according to the dying mind's insults and injuries, or its senile happiness. She went on to tell me the story, which I have forgotten. And then we—what's the romantic expression? We fell into each other's arms and slept.

Forty miles below Koblenz, in the Rhine Gorge, where, on a granite cliff, Lorelei once caused ships to founder and men to drown, she received an e-mail message from her brother: *Father died unexpectedly last night. Massive stroke. Funeral Friday.*

"You'd think he was sending a telegram—he's so frugal with his words," she said; and I heard in hers a reproach that hid her grief.

"I'll turn around and head for Cologne. You can get a flight there for the States."

Jameson looked at me. I saw in her candid gaze a question, which I answered impulsively but not—as things turned out—rashly.

"I'll go with you, if you like."

She nodded, then went below to mourn or pack, or both, while I turned the boat around. Before we left it at the wharf in Cologne, I had e-mailed my resignation to the chairman of Chronos Yachts and to the beautifully dressed mannequin in Palm Beach, whose face I no longer recall.

JAMESON AND I FLEW TO AMERICA. As the plane neared the eastern seaboard, the captain began to talk over the PA system. He spoke lovingly of the sea. As a young man, he wished above all else to become a sailor. (How strange the convergences of life!) I looked out the window at the little lights shaking on the black ocean.

"Fishing boats," the captain said, as if he could read my thoughts.

The interior of the plane was dark. Jameson and the other passengers were asleep—all, that is, except me. The window was cold against my forehead. The sun was waiting for me over the brink of the western world and beyond "the Territory," which in Huck's childhood marked the limit of our imperial destiny. Behind the locked cockpit door, the captain talked softly.

"I dream," he said, "of sleeping with Madeleine, a stewardess on the Paris–New York flight. We met only once, in a small hotel on the Trocadero. We stood together at the window and looked at the Eiffel Tower. It was a moment of high romance. When the light went out of the sky, we went to bed."

He described her lingerie, her eyes, the shape of her mouth. Her hair, he said, was "like mahogany"—the color and the shine of it. He described his ecstasy as the Eiffel Tower loomed in at the window, its lights trembling against the Parisian night. The captain fell silent while the great black wings dipped. A beverage cart rolled slowly down the aisle. Then over the PA, I heard a sound like water over stones. Like rain. Like the sea. It was the sound of the captain weeping. The plane stopped, lingered in midair—a dream. I touched my forehead to the cold window, and the plane continued on to LAX.

IN CALIFORNIA, I SOUGHT AN END to movement, which had—outside of time and in it—bewildered and exhausted me. I have theorized, since returning to Hannibal like an elephant at the end of its road, that the Pacific coast summoned so many of us so that we might finally be rid of restlessness. We went, not for gold, oil, oranges, or Hollywood, but to be finished with the westering tide that began—centuries ago—in the British Isles, Europe, and in Africa (bringing Jim to me, no matter how he may have fought and suffered by it). We sought cessation at the edge of the blue ocean and relief at stopping in our tracks. Until we've stopped, how else are we ever to begin? This is what I think, and it is the case for me, who had never stopped, never truly made a start or loved or been happy until I settled by the Pacific Ocean with Jameson. Maybe that is what the book will be about: not Huck Finn's or Albert Barthelemy's journeying, but their having reached a final destination—save one.

My logbooks are entrusted to the safekeeping of my friend and executor, Marco Knauff, a Dutchman I met in Papendrecht; they might serve as an appendix for my memoir. Remind me to give you his address.

Yes, I was content to be in Santa Monica with Jameson for as long as we were together. Which was long enough for happiness, but not so long as to see happiness become like the porridge set before me with a thump on the table by Miss Watson as a punishment, the spoon tasting like tarnish, stiff in the cold gray mound. What made me happy was the perfect ordinariness of our years together. Days passed, one merging without comment into the next. She made her picture books. *The Boy in His Winter* won a Caldecott Medal. I wrote articles for a yachting magazine. My style was praised. I rode in boats, but my voyages by river or by sea were finished. We took our meals together. We watched television or read. We made love when desire summoned us. We rested, slept, and submitted to our separate dreaming on the black rivers of sleep, which never will converge. Returning, we kept those figments to ourselves, like two guilty persons surprised by what is either too precious or too disturbing to share.

Were we ever bored?

Many times. Boredom is an aspect of time, impossible to escape. (I was never bored during that aeon on the raft with Jim, because we traveled outside time, or beyond it.)

Did Jameson love me?

Who can say what another person thinks; how he or she loves or hates? Dragons nesting on their golden hoard, we guard our deepest feelings—tender or base—like a wound that secretly thrills. That is, if we are aware of them; I think the most important lie too deep for sounding. But yes, I suppose Jameson did love me. She behaved toward me like a woman who loves someone over the course of years, constantly and inconstantly. I read her feelings, even those hidden from herself, the way a pilot does a river's bars and shoals. She was sometimes warm and at other times cool as our affection waxed and waned and waxed again. So yes, all in all, Jameson loved me, and we endured.

I remember little of our nearly twenty years—shy of twenty by a little less than two. Our marriage was like a journey down an unknown river so uncommonly wide you can't see the shore. Afterward, you recall water, moving fast or slow, not much else. Let's see. I remember black umbrellas tipping rain when the mourners leaned to look at Jameson's father lowered into the raw, blackish earth. That was the beginning. And that was at the end, also—only it was Jameson's turn to disappear and mine to watch alone. My umbrella was furled; the rain had only threatened; the earth was not so black, but raw notwithstanding. But those dismal parentheses enclosed a life, which passed, for beings like us, with the speed and terrible suddenness of time.

I'll tell you something else I remember: a picture. For years and years while I was with Jameson, I had not thought of Jim or Tom Sawyer. Or if I did, they seemed figures in a childish dream. And then on an afternoon when I was going through her things—*handling* them as if they carried, like a light-sensitive emulsion, the memory of her face—I came across a book of Civil War photographs made by Brady, Gardner, Gibson, O'Sullivan, and the rest. And among those taken at Vicksburg, was one of Jim in front of a white tent, fixed forever in time and space. And the black and formless shape (a smudge of shadow) caught in the tent flaps' narrow darkness must be Huck. Must be *I*. I tell you it has to be! I recalled how the photographer had shooed me inside, to shuffle nervously among dead men stacked in waiting for the cart. The photographer had wanted only Jim for his wet-plate negative. He may have chosen him for no other reason than the picturesque effect of a black man posed against a white tent. But by an accident of color and falling light, Jim's existence had been confirmed, while Huck's—mine—had not. The picture unnerved by recalling me to the long-vanished past while, at the same time, it caused me to doubt it. In panic, I came near to forsaking Albert Barthelemy for Huckleberry Finn!

I stayed in the apartment where Jameson and I had lived, with its view of the Pacific Ocean, which in Huck's time had been America's manifest destiny. (Because the nation's impressionable years coincided with my own, its destiny may well be mine. If this is true, I've spent 240-odd years trying to evade it.) You may think me like the starling, which appropriates the home laboriously carved from a dead tree by the industrious woodpecker. But I was jealous of the place where she'd lived. She lingered yet in the curtains, the wardrobe, the drawers, in the spoon she used to stir her tea. Even now, so very many years later, I can hear its pleasant clatter against the bone of china cup and saucer blooming with mauve roses.

So I stayed on, writing boat reviews and collecting, as her assignee, royalties from her picture books, which did well, especially "ours"; I mean *The Boy in His Winter*, whom I was fast becoming. Like a loose tooth we wiggle in the gum—half in fear of pain, half for the pleasure it incites—I would read it during days of nostalgia or self-pity. It's gone, that book; I don't know where I lost it. I wonder if it's in print anymore. I still have Jameson's book about the giraffe. Remember, I recited the first page. The last went like this: *"I see a giraffe, standing at the edge of the world. On one side is the night. But he is not looking at the darkness. He faces the light that is spilling over the earth's shining edge. See how he is standing in it?" Mother and Father looked. And they saw Rupert. They saw him wading in a flood of golden sunshine as the sun began to rise.* I like to think it was Albert who was looking at Rupert, whose name might as well have been Jim. Do you know I'd forgotten what Jim looked like? If it weren't for the photo of him at Vicksburg, he would have vanished forever. My past had haunted me and then, what's worse, it deserted me.

I tried once to write a book of my own: a time-travel novel, of all things. But I couldn't imagine a machine to shuttle between the tenses as gorgeously as Wells's had. So I gave it up and, turning seventy, stopped writing for the magazine and yielded entirely to stillness. I could no longer afford the apartment with its view of the ocean, and found a cheaper one in town, on Euclid Street near Fourteenth. I smiled to think what Jim and Tom would say if they knew I'd arrived, at last, in Mexico, even if it was only "Little." I frittered away time, happy to squander that element which had figured even more than water in my life and its story.

I dawdled in the streets of Little Mexico, drinking *cervezas* or Mexican sodas on the corners with people whose faces looked as if they'd been shaped from red clay and earth. I loved them, though I suspect they merely humored me. They called me Señor Alberto, and the young women flirted because they found me comical. I did so myself. There were no rivers left for me, and I came no nearer to the ocean than the end of Santa Monica Pier, which I visited at night to be still amid a moving crowd, listening to tender words or unkind ones, or to the popular music of the time as I had, in an earlier age, to the songs of Stephen Foster or the shameful tunes of minstrelsy. I stood on the end of the pier, like Rupert at the edge of the world, and watched fishermen dream of once more lifting into the gaudy light Pacific mackerel, bonito, halibut, and thornbacks—banished sadly and forever from the animal kingdom. I never held a rod again, or a woman either, except, in farce, a brazen señorita in the Euclid Street Laundromat.

I became a tourist on the Internet. I would sit at my computer, poring over satellite maps of—what else? Rivers! In my room in Little Mexico, I went over every stretch of fresh or brackish water I had known, beginning with the Mississippi and ending on the Rhine. Next, I sought out rivers I did not, and would not, ever know: the Nile, Orinoco, Volga, Zambezi, ancient Tigris, golden Mekong, labyrinthine Amazon. There are many rivers, and I spent months and years on them, seeing them as roving satellites must and—at the limit of magnification—as I would have, standing on their heights. My delight was to edge up, by degrees, until—suddenly—the river revealed its vessels to me: stolid tugs on the Hudson, coal barges on the Danube, oil tankers on the Jordan, dhows leaving the Indus for the Indian Ocean, junks tacking on the Perfume River, fragrant with fallen blossoms, past the tombs of the Nguyễn emperors.

Hunting for rivers, I happened on a map site called

Minkowski—.org or .net—I don't remember which, and it doesn't matter, because it proved to be a phantom of the Internet: there one day and gone the next. I used it to look at the Mississippi at Hannibal and—magnifying the river— the town came into view as it had been in the past. *My* past. I saw Hannibal as it had been in 1835! Muff Potter's shack and Pap's squatting on the mud, Marie Laveau's place in the pine woods, houses belonging to Miss Watson and the Widow Douglas, Aunt Polly, Judge Thatcher, the Phelpses, and the Wilkses, the jailhouse, circulating library, church, schoolhouse, the granite works and the sawmill, the square with the granite monument to the War of Independence, which Tom and I had desecrated with broken eggs the night before Halloween—my last in town.

You say you don't believe it?

Haven't you learned by now how fantastic a business it is to be alive? Haven't I told you even more wonderful and strange things than this?

Restless, I walked past Euclid Park, down Colorado to Ocean Avenue and the pier. I stood at its end, looking out to sea, at the lights trembling in the darkness. I remembered a vanished night on the Hooghly River when the search-lights had swept the black water for bodies of the floating dead. Squinting the way I did when I wanted to bring the invisible into view, I thought I saw Tom Sawyer, Jim, and Huck Finn, like bundles on the water, navigating silently for home, according to hydrology. The carrousel was turning musically behind me on its axis, making an eternal figure in the night as surely as the wheeling stars. The time had come round for me to go home.

AND SO I CAME TO BE, ONCE MORE, in Hannibal after a 235-year absence. The year was not 1835. The Web site, fugitive as it had been, was not a time machine. It couldn't restore or reprise the past. Its gift was one of retrospection—for an old man, a greater marvel. For old men—and women, too, for all I know of them—the glance is always backward. What is there to see ahead, except for the unmentionable destination? Unless the Widow Douglas had been right and is, at this moment, shaking a tambourine in heaven—unlike that harridan Miss Watson, who's in the oven, broiling.

Can you guess what I did first on the afternoon of my arrival? No? I bought this—my corncob pipe. I'm forbidden to smoke it. My heart, you know. But I suckle it, tasting, like a child the milk of its mother's breast, a rich residue of tobacco tar. I intend to have it burned with me: I'm to be cremated—it's written in my will—and my ashes put into the Mississippi. A gorgeous joke! And my final escape from destiny, in that Twain would have had his Huck buried in consecrated ground, most likely in the Hannibal Cemetery, with a nicely chiseled stone recording the opening and closing parentheses of a normal human life. Old ironist and sinner, Twain might have installed a stone angel to weep its rust-colored tears over me, to irritate Hannibal's self-righteous folk, who considered me a nuisance and a damned soul.

Before I arrived on this chaise longue, a skinny octogenarian in bathrobe and slippers, I took my revenge—twice daily, Tuesday through Sunday—playing the role of Mark Twain, river pilot and raconteur, at the Hannibal Riverside Amusement Park. Oh, how I relished it! Can you imagine me, made up and dressed to look like him as he was when he, too, got to be old? I lived for the two hours, six times each week, when I piloted a miniature steamboat—preposterous thing!—a half league downriver and back, telling stories of Tom and Jim and Huck to passengers who seemed more interested in the ducks than in what I had to say. But I didn't care. I amused myself by playacting my nemesis, making him look ridiculous; and the stories I told were mine. Who was to know? Few people in the 2070s had read *The Adventures of Huckleberry Finn*. Have you? The fun went on for four years and a little more, until I crashed and sank *The Mark Twain*, as that silly tin-pot steamboat was called. I steered her into a snag and tore her bottom to flinders. The sun was in my eyes, and my eyes, overcast by cataracts, weren't much use to me anymore. I guess I'd seen enough for one lifetime—for three or four lifetimes, as it happens.

That cloud, high above the river—see it? It's the very same one that flew over my childhood.

This seems a good place for me to stop before lighting out for the Territory. I've had my say, and I've packed this book with life, knowing full well that life is always elsewhere.

You want to know how to finish this comedy—with what parting words?

With the same ones Mark Twain used to finish his, damn him!

THE END, YOURS TRULY, HUCK FINN.

Acknowledgments

DURING NEARLY FORTY-FIVE YEARS OF WRITING, I have been lucky to find many who have been kind to it and to me—enough, doubtless, to crowd this page with names. In the past, I have resisted the temptation to acknowledge friends and mentors, en masse, afraid to leave one or another out, because of my forgetfulness. But this seems a good time to try my hand at a comprehensive gratitude. So thanks—to my mother, who showed me the unmatched pleasure of reading, and to Mildred Osler, an English teacher who, in 1967, while students rampaged in the hall, stood, with diminutive frame but indomitable will, against the wall and recited from a novel by Thomas Hardy. My thanks to Philip Roth, who taught me how to read a story (if I remember rightly, we read, among other novels, *The Adventures of Huckleberry Finn*) and, by his example, how to behave well toward others. Thanks, also, to poets Daniel Hoffman and Phillip Booth and novelists Jerre Mangione and George P. Elliott, who treated a young man like the writer he wished to be, but wasn't yet. I've profited by the goodwill of friends like Gordon Lish, Marco Knauff, Brian Evenson, Faruk Ulay, Kate Bernheimer, Dawn Raffel, John Madera, Peter Markus, Tobias Carroll, Ed Renn, Dave Moore, and my persevering theatrical agent, Per Lauke. I've enjoyed the attentions of many editors—chief among them: George Plimpton (*The Paris Review*), Stephen Donadio and Carolyn Kuebler (*New England Review*), Celia Johnson and Maria Gagliano (*Slice*), Lee Chapman (*First Intensity*), Vincent Standley (*3rd bed*), Deron Bauman and Cooper Renner (*elimae*), Robley Wilson (*The North American Review*), Sven Birkerts and William Pierce (*AGNI*), Matt Bell (*The Collagist*), John Hennessy and Jennifer Acker (*The Common*), Richard Peabody (*Gargoyle*), Alice Whittenburg and G.S. Evans (*Café Irreal*), and Sebnem Basimi Holzer (*Visual Artbeat*). I've been fortunate in having devoted, selfless publishers like Kathryn Rantala (Ravenna Press), Eugene Lim (Ellipsis Press), Tod Thilleman (Spuyten Duyvil), Derek White (Calamari Press), R. M. Berry (FC2), J. A. Tyler (Mud Luscious Press), Christopher Gould (Broadway Play Publishing), and, on the happy occasion of *The Boy in His Winter* and *Love Among the Particles,* my estimable publisher, Erika Goldman, her Bellevue Literary Press team, Adam Beaudoin, Leslie Hodgkins, and Molly Mikolowski, the press's meticulous copyeditor, Carol Edwards, as well as the painstaking Joe Gannon. I gratefully acknowledge a debt to the National Endowment for the Arts, the Pennsylvania Council on the Arts, and, doubly, to the New Jersey Council on the Arts. And, lastly, I offer gratitude and love to Helen—for four decades my wife and friend.

The author is grateful to *The Collagist*, *Construction Magazine,* and *Slice Magazine* for publishing an excerpt from this novel.

About the Author

NORMAN LOCK's recent story collection, *Love Among the Particles*, was published in 2013 by Bellevue Literary Press. *The House of Correction* enjoyed a successful run during the 2013 theater season in Istanbul and opened in Warsaw and Athens in 2014. His latest radio play, *Mounting Panic*, premiered in 2013 in Germany. He has won *The Paris Review* Aga Kahn Prize for Fiction and the Dactyl Foundation Literary Fiction Award, and has been awarded writing fellowships from the New Jersey Council on the Arts (1999, 2013), the Pennsylvania Council on the Arts (2009), and the National Endowment for the Arts (2011).

DATE DUE

ze-winning
fit press
ersection of
erature are
xperience.
accustomed
world.
catalogue of
g.